What's Done in the Dark

A MONA BAKER NOVEL

Krys Batts

ISBN: 0692226370
ISBN 13: 9780692226377
Library of Congress Control Number: 2014909818
The Real Ideal, LLC, Dallas, TX

Cover design by Robin Ludwig Design Inc.
http://www.gobookcoverdesign.com/

Thank you to my wonderful friends and family for your critiques! This book would not exist without you.

What's Done in the Dark:
A Mona Baker Novel

The question is not only, "Who are you now?"
but also, "Who do you want to become?"

ONE

It was barely 8:30 AM, but the morning had already been long and terribly confusing to Mona Baker, whose routine had been rudely interrupted by the arrival of police brandishing a search warrant. Rather than being en route to drop off her seven-year-old daughter, Sophie, at school, she was instead seated anxiously at home, cordoned off with Sophie and her husband, Aaron, in their spacious seafoam-colored living room as three police officers wordlessly went about searching the family's residence. To prevent the Bakers from leaving either the room or the house, two more officers stood guard nearby, having grown eerily silent after firing off a round of questions that made absolutely no sense to Mona.

"Mr. Baker, do you have any illicit drugs in the house?"

"Mrs. Baker, have you ever observed your husband negotiating the exchange of drugs for payments?"

"Mrs. Baker, have you recently assisted anyone with the transport of illegal drugs?"

"Mr. Baker, do you have any guns in the house?"

Aaron's response had been one of sheer moral indignation and he had rolled his eyes while commanding Mona to remain silent until their lawyer arrived. As a high-powered executive at Exxon-Mobil, Aaron was accustomed to being in control and was fully unwilling to cede his superiority to the officers, who had instantly backed off at the mention of an attorney, maintaining weird smirks on their faces since then. It was as though they knew something that neither Aaron nor Mona knew, a notion that sickened Mona to her stomach. Aaron, on the other hand, had no problem dismissing their lowly proctors as his eyes deliberately followed the other officers' orderly movements, finally locking in on the empty doorway to the home office into which they had all disappeared. If Aaron was suspicious of why they had chosen to focus on that one room, he kept his thoughts to himself, quietly, tensely watching the doorway since he was powerless to do anything else.

And then Mona heard one of the officers call out, "Got it!" after which all three cops exited the office and headed toward Mona and Aaron. One of them was carrying a small, brown package that was tied with twine. Minutes earlier when Mona had opened the front door, he had introduced himself as Detective Harold Monroe and he appeared to be in charge. As Mona clutched Sophie tightly against her, the detective approached the couple with the dubious package in hand.

"Mr. Baker, you are under arrest for –"

"You can't arrest me!" Aaron gritted his teeth, his body angling toward the detective as he made no effort to disguise his arrogant defiance.

Detective Monroe didn't flinch. "Sir, we have just found a kilo of cocaine in your home." He turned the package to display a small incision at the top as well as the white powdery contents inside. "Are you implying that this belongs to your wife?"

"I've never seen that package before! Someone must have planted it here!"

"Well, I've never seen it before either!" Mona gasped, shocked that Aaron had failed to unequivocally refute that the drugs were hers.

The detective continued unfazed. "Why would anyone want to plant drugs in your home, Mr. Baker?"

"How should I know?" Aaron still seemed to be more indignant than concerned at the events rapidly unfolding around him and his family. "Maybe those are the types of questions that you need to start investigating, Detective, instead of treating me and my family like common criminals."

The officer merely smiled calmly. "Well, we'll see whose fingerprints turn up on this package before drawing any conclusions. How about that?" He nodded to one of the officers standing behind the sofa, a signal that prompted the officer to immediately jerk Aaron upward and off of his seat.

"What is this? I—I don't understand," Mona stammered. Her eyes darted from the arresting officer to Aaron as she folded her arms even more tightly around her frightened, sniffling child. She heard the handcuffs clink into place around Aaron's wrists and instinctively recoiled.

"Shut up, Mona!" Aaron spat at her before reeling back to face the detective.

"Lawson, read him his rights and take him to the car." Detective Monroe's apparent nonchalance further fanned Aaron's rage.

"I'm going to sue you and the City of Houston for every penny you have! You're making the biggest mistake of your life!"

"Haven't you heard, Mr. Baker? The city is broke. So go ahead and sue. I guarantee that you and your lawyer will be waiting a long time for that payday."

Following his orders, but with far less restraint than Detective Monroe exhibited, Lawson practically shoved Aaron toward the front door, reciting the Miranda rights from memory as the detective's emotionless gaze now fell on Mona and Sophie. "Mrs. Baker, you need to come with me."

—m—

"Mrs. Baker, can you explain why your fingerprints are on the package of cocaine that we seized from your house this morning?" Detective Monroe coolly leaned against the back of his wooden chair, arms crossed, hard brown eyes never shifting from Mona's face as his partner, Nate O'Bryan, stood observing from a corner of the small, brightly lit interrogation room.

Apparently apathetic, Mona raised a cigarette to her lips and inhaled deeply. "We've already been over that several times, Detective." Smoke escaped her mouth as she spoke. She then blew the remaining fog in her lungs directly toward Harold's face on the other side of the table between them. Mona had insisted on popping a valium pill before leaving the house and it was clearly doing its job all too well for his liking.

"We're going over it again." Harold didn't budge even though he detested the idea of breathing the secondhand smoke. It was a shame, really, that someone as attractive as Mrs. Baker had acquired such a disgusting habit. Although he knew her to be African-American as he was, she could easily pass for Hispanic. Her hair was long, dark, and straight, her facial features fine, petite build, large dark brown eyes. And dressed in a black Versace suit, she looked like she should've been sitting in a board room instead of here with him for questioning.

"As I've said several times already, my fingerprints can't possibly be on the package because I've never seen it before this morning." She lightly tapped her cigarette against an ashtray, raised it to her lips for another drag, and then looked at her watch. It was obvious that her impatience was growing. For over three hours, Harold and Nate had pummeled her with overtly threatening questions despite their year-long surveillance of the Bakers having already proven that she had not been involved with any illegal drug operations. But they still needed to get her statements on the record. More importantly, they also needed this chance to intimidate Mona, the goal being to eventually elicit her gratitude for the deal they planned to offer in exchange for her testimony against her husband. It was a strategy that seemed to be falling woefully flat. "I also did not know that my husband is a suspected drug pusher."

"And you really expect me to believe that?" Harold shook his head with dismay. "After eight years of marriage, you actually expect me and my partner here to buy that you didn't know that your husband has been trafficking drugs between Mexico and Houston for at least the past ten years. Jees. You must really take us for idiots." For the first time in several minutes, Harold turned to shoot an incredulous look at Nate, who appeared equally as baffled. "You are really a piece of work, you know that?"

"She's not just a piece of work, man," Nate spoke up with a show of animosity as he moved toward the table. "She's the worst kind of loser and she's going to wind up in prison just like her husband." Nate stopped at the edge of the table, one hand on his hip, the other stroking his short, brownish-blond hair before pointing a finger in Mona's face. "You'd better start talking, lady, cuz, believe me, you don't wanna know what happens to rich girls like you in prison." His eyes locked with Mona's as she continued smoking, apparently devoid of any emotions. "And what do you think is gonna happen to that little girl of yours, huh? Well, let me paint the picture for ya. She's gonna end up in a foster home somewhere, in a regular barnyard full of other kids that nobody wants, probably lucky if she even graduates from high school."

"That's enough, Nate! Back off and let me handle this." Harold waved his hand toward Nate, but his eyes never left Mona's face. It seemed as if nothing penetrated her stony facade, which was unusual for women, particularly mothers who were naturally afraid of losing their children as she had to be. From what they had all observed over the past year, Mrs. Baker was an excellent, loving mother. But as yet, they had entirely failed to tap into that emotion. "I'll ask again, Mrs. Baker. How do you explain having no knowledge of your husband's illegal drug activities?"

Nate was back in his corner with a foot resting against the wall as he and Mona continued staring at each other, his eyes smoldering, her eyes vacant. Finally, Mona restored her attention to Harold as more smoke wafted from her lips. "Detective, my husband and I aren't exactly on the closest of terms. He tells me nothing about his affairs."

"Uh huh. Right. So how did you think he was paying for that mansion that you live in? How do think he could afford the Mercedes that you drive? Sure, he makes a good living as a vice-president at Exxon-Mobil, but he's been living the lifestyle of a CEO. How could you explain that?"

"Good investments. Why would I think anything else?" Mona extinguished the cigarette in the ashtray. She then withdrew a new one from the pack, lit it, and took a drag.

"You've never asked your husband how he's managed to *invest* so well all these years?"

"No. Like I said, we're not close. I live well, my daughter lives well. That's all I care about."

"So you don't care about your husband?"

"No, I don't."

"Then why are you married to him?"

"For the money, detective. And years ago for the sex." She exhaled more fog and shrugged. "We used to have great sex. When we met, I was very young, poor, and inexperienced."

"Yes, I'm familiar with your background. You were born and raised in one of the worst slums in the city. But you sure did make out well, didn't you? Married a rich guy, masqueraded as a soccer mom while helping him transport drugs into Houston..."

"For the last time, I was not involved with any of this drug business. If you insist on accusing me of being a drug dealer, then I will insist on my attorney joining us before I say another word."

"Okay, Mrs. Baker. Okay." Harold leaned forward, resting his elbows and forearms on the table, pausing for a moment, still watching closely. He had no choice but to halt the line of questioning, which had done nothing to raze her rocklike dispassion. He'd have to be more direct. "Let's say that I believe you. Would you be willing to help us prosecute your husband by giving your testimony in court?"

"What would I testify to? I've already told you that I know absolutely nothing about any drug business."

"That's true. But you can testify to the fact that certain people we can prove have been involved with the trafficking have also been visitors at your home on numerous occasions over the past eight years. You can testify that there have been clear relationships between these individuals and your husband." Met with stark silence and a blank stare, Harold continued. "There's also one other matter that we need your help with."

"And what is that?" Mona was beginning to bristle now.

"We need any financial records that your husband may have that prove the drug-related income. The bank account records that we've already secured from your house are clean, which means that he has another account somewhere that we haven't found, probably under a different name."

"I have no idea where it could be!"

"We think that you do know. Maybe you don't even realize it. You could've overheard your husband mention a foreign bank account to someone. Or maybe you've seen bank statements around the house for accounts that you didn't know about."

"I've neither seen nor heard anything, Detective. And I'm not agreeing to testify against my husband. If your accusations are correct, which I'm still not convinced they are, I'd be dead before I could reach the witness stand." He noticed that her hand trembled as she raised her cigarette to her lips. "You don't know him like I do. He can be extremely violent."

"We can protect you. We'll put you and your daughter in a safe house until the trial." Finally! She had cracked.

"You can't protect us," Mona huffed. "You're nothing compared to Aaron. Do you understand how well connected he is? The man has lunch with the mayor several times a month and is on very friendly terms with the governor. He's untouchable." She exhaled a long stream of smoke. "You're all fools, Detective. Plain fools."

"So you're refusing to help us." Harold was unmoved. Everyone involved with the bust was already well aware of Aaron's social alliances.

"That's correct. I won't risk my life or my daughter's life for this ridiculous investigation of yours."

"Then how about saving your sister's life?" It was time to play the card that Harold had been holding, an ace he felt certain.

"Don't be stupid. My sister has been dead for nearly ten years. You've got nothing you can use to manipulate me. I know how you people work."

Harold reached down and grabbed a large envelope that had been leaning against his chair. As Mona watched, he opened the envelope, removed several eight-by-ten black and white photos, and placed them in front of Mona, who remained motionless. "Go ahead. Look at 'em. I think you'll find them very interesting."

"No. I think I'll leave instead. You obviously have no grounds to arrest me or you would have done so already." She placed her hands against the edge of the table and began pushing her chair back.

"If I were you, I wouldn't leave before I looked at those pictures."

"But you're not me."

"Yeah, and your sister ain't dead."

"You don't know what you're talking about!"

"Look at the photos, Mrs. Baker."

Mona glared at Harold for several long seconds before finally allowing her gaze to roll downward to the photos in front of her. The picture on top was a close-up shot of a lithe woman wearing shades and a light trench coat. Mona slowly, reluctantly set aside the photo to view the next one in the small stack. This one showed the same woman standing on a street corner in front of a red brick building and her face was more clearly visible. She had somewhat slanted eyes, full lips, and skin the shade of cocoa.

Mona slid the second photo away to view another one. Her eyes seemed to have stopped blinking as she stared at the woman, who was crossing the street of some city. Rather than go on to the next photo, Mona straightened the stack of pictures and pushed them to the middle of the table toward Harold. "This woman is not my sister." She took an extremely long drag on her cigarette. But while her gaze was in Harold's direction, she seemed to be looking right through him.

"It's her, Mrs. Baker. And I can tell that you know it is." Harold allowed the photos to remain where Mona had left them. "Are you sure you don't want to see the rest of the pictures? They're quite convincing evidence that your sister never came to any harm as you and your family believed."

"Detective, anyone can doctor photos. My seven-year-old daughter could do a better job on our computer at home." She exhaled more smoke. "I assume that I'm free to go now." Her hand was trembling more noticeably and she had begun tapping her foot on the white linoleum floor.

"I can understand your position, Mrs. Baker. I wouldn't expect you to believe that Simone is alive without seeing her for yourself. That's why I've arranged your reunion." Harold stood up. "Come with me."

Mona's eyes grew to the size of saucers as both Nate and Harold walked to the door and opened it. Once Nate had exited the room, Harold turned back around to see Mona still seated in stunned silence. "Are you coming?"

Mona considered the question before determinedly jutting out her chin and jamming her cigarette into the ashtray. She stood and walked to the door, stopping to levelly face Harold. "You'll see. Whoever you've brought here is not my sister."

—⁓—

With Nate and Mona following closely behind, Harold approached the door to another interrogation room located a few paces down the hallway from the room in which Mona had been sequestered. Harold opened the door and spoke to someone that Mona couldn't yet see. "I have a visitor here for you." He stepped aside to let Mona pass him and enter the room.

Mona's feet felt more like boulders. They didn't want to move. And her mind did not want to process the possibility of who may be inside the room. Nevertheless, she moved slowly forward and halted inside the doorway. The woman from the photos was standing in a corner furthest away from the entrance. She was wearing a powder blue pantsuit, her black hair neatly groomed in a sheik hairstyle that left little to comb. Her arms were crossed and tracks of tears had streaked her makeup. When her eyes met Mona's, fresh tears began to fall. "Mona, I'm sorry. I'm so sorry." She cautiously walked toward Mona and stopped a few feet away. "I know you thought I was dead and I've wanted to see you so many times, but I was afraid you'd hate me now." She wiped at the tears flowing down her cheeks and then moved to hug Mona, who abruptly stepped backward to avoid the woman's touch.

"Who are you?" Mona's voice was cold and her mind was reeling. "Why are you doing this?" She looked like Simone, her voice sounded the way she remembered her sister's voice, but it could not be her. Simone, who was two years younger than Mona, had disappeared years ago at age sixteen and never been heard from again, utterly destroying both Mona's and their mother's lives. Although Simone's body had never been found, everyone naturally assumed that she had to be dead because she would never have left of her own volition without telling someone. Horrible scenarios of death being inflicted on a helpless Simone had plagued all of their minds and grief poisoned every aspect of their lives. Finally, their mother's broken heart had simply given out on her and at the unbelievably young age of thirty-nine she had died in her sleep within a year of Simone's disappearance. And Mona had been left alone at age nineteen. It had been the worst year of her life, the agony of it choking her even now, nine years later. And so Simone couldn't still be alive. She couldn't. Mona's body went numb as she examined the woman from head to toe, searching for proof that an imposter stood before her.

Seeming confused at Mona's reaction, the woman looked to Harold and Nate. "But...I thought you told her. Didn't you tell her?"

"We told her, but she didn't believe us." A smirk lined Nate's face as he watched Mona's stoic demeanor completely disintegrate.

"We'll leave you two alone for a few minutes so you can talk." Harold tapped Nate's arm and they left the room, closing the door behind them.

The woman reached for Mona's hand, which jerked backwards, nearly hitting the doorknob to again avoid her touch. With sagging shoulders, she then walked to a chair and took a seat as Mona, still frozen by the door, wordlessly watched. The women stared at each other for a few moments, scrutinizing one another.

Mona again grudgingly admitted to herself that the person seated before her bore an impossibly familiar resemblance to her sister, who shared very few of Mona's physical characteristics. They had been fathered by different men, both of whom virtually disappeared upon learning that Beatrice, their mother, was pregnant. Thanks to Beatrice's unfailingly poor taste in men, Simone's father had been a drug addict while Mona's father had been locked up in prison on and off for most of his life, having chosen to burglarize homes and storefronts for money rather than getting a job. And so it had been the three of them, the women, fending for themselves and barely making ends meet. Beatrice held down three low-paying jobs and Mona, forced to mature very quickly, watched over Simone behind bolted doors and thickly curtained windows. Although their mother's brother, Uncle Clarence, had tried his best to represent a father figure, the women had mostly relied on each other. To say the least, times had been tough in their crime-ridden neighborhood. They all had heard the bullets that gangs fired at night on their street and they had fervently prayed that the doors and walls would hold the criminals at bay. A way out, they believed, had to be coming because Beatrice was determined that her daughters would go to college and one day save them all with better paying jobs than she could ever secure. Each of them had held on to this dream like a lifeline, hoping for a safer, abundant future that certainly seemed possible – until Simone had disappeared.

"You look good, Mona. Beatrice woulda been proud." Silence. "It is me, ya know. Simone. I know you're having a hard time believing that. Or maybe you just don't wanna believe it, but it's true." She looked away toward a wall. "You remember when we used to go outside when it rained and catch live crawfish? We'd put 'em in buckets and take 'em inside the house. 'Course, Beatrice wouldn't let us keep 'em. She always made us take 'em back out and dump the crawfish in the gutter." She smiled slightly and turned back to face Mona. "Remember?"

Mona remained perfectly still, her eyes following every gesture the woman made, her ears listening closely to the words emitted from her mouth. She remembered the crawfish well. She also remembered how Mama shooed them out of the house with their overflowing buckets. Other than Mama and Simone, Mona could think of no one else who would have known about any of that.

The woman's facial expression changed, becoming serious and pained. "Do you remember when you got your first job? I was fourteen and Beatrice was workin' the same three jobs she'd had since forever. You and me, we hardly saw her except on Sundays. Then you started workin' and I was at home by myself most of the time after school." She took a shaky breath as more tears began to pour from her eyes. She closed them and pursed her lips in a grimace before continuing. "That's when Uncle Clarence started comin' 'round more. He told Beatrice that he was lookin' in on me, but that wasn't the whole truth." A soft moan escaped her and her chest began to heave as she struggled to go on. "Mona, he wasn't just checkin' on me. He was...He was raping me." A waterfall of tears flowed from her eyes and her hands flew to her face to quickly wipe them away as she struggled to continue in a tremulous voice. "He raped me almost every day. Every day! I would scream and kick and scratch, but nothin' would get him off of me! I was so scared! And I hated him! I was just a kid. I trusted him. Why would he do that to me? Why?" The woman's voice had become an excruciating wail and she was finally too overcome to speak as the sobs racked her body.

Suddenly, Mona realized that she was also crying. Erupting with emotion, she rushed toward the woman and wrapped her arms around her, convinced that Simone was indeed still alive and sitting with her, both of them overwhelmed with tears for several moments.

Simone finally continued between shaky breaths, pulling away to see Mona's face. "I told Beatrice what he was doin' to me, but she didn't believe me. I didn't know what to do."

"Why didn't you tell me?" Mona's voice sounded raspy to her own ears. She could hardly get the words out as she clutched Simone's shoulders, squeezing them to reassure herself that her sister was truly with her, real flesh.

"What would you have done? You couldn't do anything to help me, Mona."

"We could have gone to the police."

"And risk Beatrice bein' declared unfit? You and me woulda been put in foster homes, separated. What kinda life would that have been?"

Mona reflected on Nate's comment about Sophie. "Yeah. But what you did, disappearing, was no better."

"It was the only thing I could do. Don't you understand? After two years of fightin' him, I couldn't take it no more. It was either leave or die."

"Oh God. I wish I had known." Her breath was a long sigh as she looked down. "And I can't believe that Mama didn't help you."

"I don't think Beatrice was willin' to lose the only person she thought was tryin' to help us."

"But that still doesn't make it right." Mona was becoming angry now, understanding that Mama had died from guilt, not a broken heart. The heartache that Mona had felt about Mama for so many years was rapidly being replaced with fury at her sister's plight. "I swear, if I had known that Uncle Clarence was doing that to you, I would have killed him! He's lucky that he's already dead." Someone had shot Uncle Clarence and burglarized his apartment the same year Simone had disappeared. At the time, Mona had been devastated to lose her last connection to her mother, but there was no emotion in her now that she knew that the man had been a child molester. He had gotten off easy.

"Yes, we're a lot alike." Simone clutched Mona's hands and peered earnestly into her eyes. "It was me who shot Uncle Clarence."

"You?" Mona was shocked. She cupped her sister's face in her hands. "No, no. It was some crazy burglar, not you. Please, not you."

"Yes, Mona. And I'm glad I did it. He needed killin'. The dirty bastard ruined my life! And I'll tell you somethin' else. I'm not sorry that Beatrice died either."

"How could you say that?"

"Because as far as I'm concerned, she handed my body over to him on a silver platter." Simone's lips quivered, but her eyes were icy, the tears having completely ceased.

Mona released a great breath and stood up to pace around the table. She couldn't fault Simone for her feelings. She probably would have felt the same way if she had been victimized by Clarence and called a liar by Mama. "Do the police know what you did?" She was already certain that they did. Harold had asked if she would cooperate to save her sister. Now she knew the deal – either cooperate or Simone would be prosecuted for murder.

"Yeah, they seem to know most of it."

"But I don't understand. How did they find you? How did they find out that you killed Uncle Clarence?"

"It's all my fault. I've been drivin' by your house for months tryin' to get up the nerve to ring the doorbell. I even got outta my car a few times, stood at the gate in your driveway, then chickened out and left. I didn't know the cops were stakin' out your house and Harold

24

said they became suspicious and started followin' me a few months ago. Next thing I know, I'm bein' apprehended this mornin' and held in this room until you could get here."

"Why would they arrest you? They still couldn't know that you killed Uncle Clarence."

"I've been thinkin' about that. Harold said that my and Clarence's fingerprints were the only ones on all the trashed furniture in Clarence's apartment and on his wallet, which made me a suspect. But they weren't able to match anyone with my prints since I'd never been arrested before. I guess they put two and two together when they figured out that your supposedly dead sister kept showin' up at your house."

"But that still doesn't explain how they obtained your fingerprints to match with Uncle Clarence's place. They would have needed your prints before they could drag you here."

"Yeah, well, I don't have all the answers. I just know that somethin' weird is going on here because they said I don't need a lawyer and I'm not formally under arrest. They haven't even asked me any questions. They just told me what they think happened to Clarence and then they said you would be here to see me. Why do you think they haven't stuck me in a jail cell yet?"

"Because they're using you to get to me." Mona sank onto the seat by her sister and hung her head.

"What do ya mean?"

"They want me to testify against my husband if he's put on trial for drug trafficking. They knew I wouldn't do it unless they had some sort of bargaining chip to force me. You're it." Mona's spirit was withered and the weakness was in her voice.

"I won't let them do that." Simone resolutely stood up and walked toward the door. "I'm ready to pay for what I did. They can't use me if I don't let 'em."

"No, Simone. I don't want you to do that. We've lost enough time as it is. I can't lose you again. The detectives were right to assume that I would feel this way."

"But would you be riskin' your life by testifyin'? I mean, is your husband involved with the mob or somethin'?"

"Honestly, I don't know who he's working with." Mona sighed and rubbed her forehead.

"But you do think the police are right about him?"

"I have no idea. Aaron and I don't talk to each other much these days. I did suspect that he was using drugs because of his unpredictable mood swings, but I would never have thought that Aaron was actually selling them. It's hard to believe that he'd be so stupid regardless of what the police are saying." She grabbed Simone's hand and attempted to smile reassuringly. "If it's true, my helping the police will be dangerous for me, but you and I lived with danger every day of our lives when we were kids. And it's worth it if I can have you back in my life. We have a lot of catching up to do."

"Mona, I don't want to go to prison, but I'd never forgive myself if anything happened to you because you were tryin' to help me. I've always known that killin' that scumbag could catch up to me and I'll take my medicine if I have to."

"Please, let's just get on with our lives and promise to be there for each other. Okay?" She hugged Simone tightly. "I love you so much and I'm just grateful to have a second chance with you."

"I love you, too, Mona." A worried frown that Mona couldn't see was etched across Simone's face. "And I promise that nothing will separate us again."

Just then, the door opened and both Harold and Nate returned to the room, closing the door behind them. "Well, well, well, what have we here? Looks like a family reunion to me."

Mona ignored Nate, released Simone, and looked directly at Harold. "Okay. You can have what you want. And I want our agreement in writing for my attorney's review."

Harold stood before her with his hands on his hips, a toothy smile pasted from ear to ear. "I expected you to say that."

TWO

"So that there's no confusion, Mrs. Baker, our agreement is null and void if you fail to hold up your part of the bargain. Is that understood?"

Mona glared at Harold, who was once again sitting across from her in the interrogation room. Nate had resumed his post in the corner and their captain, Carmen Perez, was standing beside Harold. Mona's high-priced attorney, Richard Wilkes, had also joined them and was seated next to Mona. "Understood. And so that you are clear, Detective, your department is to leave my sister alone. She's been through enough."

"Mrs. Baker," Captain Perez broke in, "we understand your concern for your sister and I want to personally assure you that we have no interest in her as long as you help us put your husband away as you've agreed to do."

Mona looked from Captain Perez to Harold before meeting her attorney's gaze and nodding her head.

"Well, everyone, I believe that our business regarding this matter is concluded." Richard made a stiff show of closing and locking his briefcase on top of the table. "Now, we'd like to know when my client will be able to see her husband."

"Not before tomorrow morning," the captain responded matter-of-factly. "We're still processing him."

"Very well. And my client's sister is free to leave with her, correct?"

"So long as she doesn't leave the city before the trial, Mr. Wilkes. She's our insurance. I'm sure you understand."

"Miss Edwards will reside with my client unless you are otherwise informed." Richard looked at Mona, his eyes briefly questioning whether she had any additional concerns. Seeing no indications from her, he stood up and motioned for Mona to accompany him to the door. "Thank you all for your time. We'll be in touch if a need arises."

"Mrs. Baker," Harold stood at the table. "We'll be in touch real soon."

The detective's statement sounded more like a veiled threat, but at this point Mona had neither the energy nor the gumption to respond. Instead, she made a fast exit with Richard and began walking down the hall toward the room in which her daughter and Simone were now waiting.

"I hope you know what you're getting yourself into," Richard spoke in a lowered voice once they were comfortably out of everyone's earshot. Standing well over six feet in height, he had to lean down to make sure Mona, who stood at 5'4", heard him. "The people your husband is accused of working with are heartless killers." They had obtained more information about Aaron's supposed business associates from the police when Mona's expected testimony was discussed. "You'd better think about holing up somewhere until the trial."

"Don't worry about me." Mona patted his portly abdomen affectionately. "I'll figure something out." For Richard's benefit, she sounded more confident than she actually felt. After years spent in an acrimonious, even at times abusive marriage, Mona was well-practiced at hiding her emotions. The truth was that she was nervous enough to vomit, but she wasn't nervous for her own sake. Rather, her greatest concern was centered on her daughter's welfare. Mona was not prepared to entrust Sophie's care to someone else if she were locked up as Aaron had been earlier that morning. No one else could possibly love and devote themselves to Sophie as she did.

"Do you need any help? I could put you in touch with someone."

"Thanks, Richard. I'll take you up on that offer if I need to."

They reached the door to the room that Simone and Sophie occupied. "Then be careful, Mona. I suggest that you grow eyes in the back of your head."

Despite her anxiety, Mona was unwilling to trust Richard, who had always appeared to be a loyal friend to Aaron. While their relationship may have been purely professional, she had no way to be sure. She had even been reluctant to contact him for his assistance with the police due to the possibility that he may not keep their client-attorney conversations confidential. Then she realized that it ultimately didn't matter since Aaron would soon learn of her deal with the police anyway. If he didn't first hear about it from his defense attorney or the cops, he would be hearing about it tomorrow morning when Mona was able to see him. Although she could barely stand the sight of him, she had to know if there was any truth to the police's allegations.

"Mommy!" Sophie jumped off her chair and ran into Mona's arms when she entered the room. "I thought you forgot about me."

"Well, you were wrong. I could never forget about my little munchkin." She leaned down and kissed the top of Sophie's head. Such a pretty little girl, possessing long, wavy, auburn-colored hair, light brown eyes, fair skin. The true product of parents with melting pot heritages, although the truth was that Aaron, whose lineage included German and Italian among others, was not her biological father. To this day, of course, he had been denied any knowledge of Sophie's illegitimacy, but Mona had known as soon as she'd first seen her baby. Monogamy had been an unrealistic, lofty marriage vow for Mona, who was not prone to love any man after witnessing the way men had carelessly discarded her mother. Rather than seeking emotional bonds, Mona kept love out of the equation when dealing with men much the way she felt that men remained detached when dealing with women. She had enjoyed her fair share of extramarital adventures as discreetly as possible, all the while certain that Aaron's infidelities were equally as voluminous, particularly within the past year. These days, he thought nothing of flaunting his disloyalty, taking calls from his nameless concubines in Mona's presence and failing to come home several nights each week. It was as though he wanted to provoke Mona, but his efforts were like waving a red flag in front of a sleeping bull. She could not have cared less if Aaron never came home again so long as she still had access to his money. For that, she would endure and overlook just about anything. If only the police would be so accommodating.

"So did you have fun with Mommy's friend, Simone, while you waited for me?"

"Yes." Sophie nodded her head without removing it from Mona's abdomen.

"She's a very sweet girl." Simone crossed the room and lightly squeezed Sophie's shoulder, eliciting a giggle in response from the child.

Mona squatted down to be eye level with Sophie. "Sophie, what would you say if I told you that Simone is Mommy's sister? Would you be happy about that?"

"Your sister?" Sophie looked from Mona to Simone, then back at Mona.

"That's right. You've seen pictures of her around Mommy's bedroom, remember?"

Sophie nodded her head. "Did God send her back from heaven for being bad?"

Mona laughed. "No, honey. God sent her back because He knew that Mommy needed her. But we can talk about that some more later, okay?"

"Okay."

"Right now, I want to make sure you understand something. Because Simone is Mommy's sister, that means that she's your aunt. Like Daddy's sister, Cheryl, is your aunt. Does that make sense?"

"I guess so." She looked at Simone, who smiled down at her.

"So what does that mean you're going to call her? Not Simone, but..."

"Aunt Simone." Sophie buried her face in Mona's neck.

"That's right, sweetie. Aunt Simone." Mona stood up and took one of Sophie's hands. "Now, are you ready to go home and eat? I'll bet you're hungry."

"Trust me," Simone interrupted, "there's no way this girl is hungry. All the police in the buildin' have been feedin' and spoilin' her the whole time we've been in here. I've never felt so invisible," she laughed.

"Oh really!" Mona smiled at Sophie. "You are certainly a charmer!"

"No, I'm not!" She giggled again.

"So you say." Mona looked toward the doorway and realized that Richard was politely waiting to escort them all out. "Sophie, say hello to Mr. Wilkes."

"Hello, Mr. Wilkes."

"Why, hello, Sophie." His voice was warm and inviting as he stepped forward to gently shake Sophie's small hand. "It's a pleasure to see you again."

"And this is my sister, Simone."

"Ah, the much talked about Miss Edwards. Pleased to make your acquaintance." He now shook Simone's hand with a much firmer grip.

"Thank you. We appreciate your help today."

"No thanks necessary. It's what I'm here to do." He moved back to the door. "I'm sure that you're all ready to leave."

Sophie tugged at Mona's hand. "Mommy, is Daddy coming home with us?"

"No, Daddy is still talking to the police, but he should be home tomorrow."

Thankfully, the answer seemed to satisfy the child, at least for the moment. Richard gestured toward the door. "Ladies?"

"Yes, thank you, Richard," Mona responded as everyone headed for the door. "If I never see the inside of this place again, it will be too soon."

―⁕―

"I'm exhausted." Relieved to be back at home, Mona was sitting with Simone at a dining table. Multiple open containers of Chinese food were scattered around the table, the contents having been devoured by the sisters. Mona rubbed her stomach and rested a leg on an empty chair. With her belly so overstuffed, she was eternally grateful that Sophie had learned to bathe herself without being supervised. At that very moment, her daughter was splashing in a bubble-filled tub, after which she would be put to bed.

"I could use a drink." Simone glanced up toward the kitchen. "Got some red wine by chance?"

"Ooh, that sounds good. I think there's a bottle in the frig. Pour me a glass?"

"Sure." Simone went into the kitchen and started opening cabinets until she located wine glasses.

As Simone poured the wine, Mona grappled with a patchwork of strong emotions – anger, joy, grief, bewilderment, confusion – that the day's events had roused within her. Her husband was a drug trafficker, her lifestyle was being threatened, her daughter's security was under assault, and her sister was alive. Her sister was here and alive! In one day, the police had introduced huge changes into Mona's life, one of them beyond wonderful, but all others stirring fears that she thought had been entirely averted when she married Aaron, a man she had believed was the exact opposite of those that her mother had chosen. Their marriage had been far from perfect, but at least Mona had thought that her greatest fear was effectively alleviated: desolate poverty. Now it was possible that Aaron's guise had been nothing more than a sham. And not only did she stand to lose everything, but Sophie's safety might be at risk. Ultimately, Mona and Simone would have to decide how to protect themselves if it came down to it. But for now, if only for tonight, she wanted to revive her bond with Simone, to know everything she could learn about her beloved sister.

"Tell me what you've been doing, how you've been living for the past ten years."

"I think we should talk about what you're gonna do tomorrow instead." Simone placed the filled wine glasses on the dining table. "We can talk about the past any time."

"No, I want to know what's happened in your life. I mean, did you go to college? Did you get married? Do you have a job? Tell me!" Mona took a sip of the wine as Simone sat back down.

"Okay, if you insist." Simone drank a healthy portion of her serving and then leaned back in her chair, closing her eyes for a moment before talking again. "Well, for starters, when I left Beatrice's house, I was sixteen and jobless, as you know. So the first things I had to figure out were where to live and how to support myself. I hitched a ride outta the city and lived on the streets in Galveston for a couple of weeks. I needed money fast so I made a decision that I'm not proud of." She paused and looked at Mona before lowering her eyes to the wineglass. "I hooked for a few months."

"Hooked? As in prostitution?" Mona was instantly filled with shock and remorse. "Oh no."

"Yeah, well, I didn't like it either, but it enabled me to eat, to pay for a pretty sleazy hotel room so I could sleep and bathe. I was fed, I was clean, I was survivin' doin' the only thing I knew – gettin' screwed."

Mona closed her eyes and inhaled a deep breath. She needed a cigarette so she reached for her purse, dug the pack out, and lit one.

"Want me to go on?"

"Yes, please. I need to know." She exhaled smog, blowing it away from Simone's direction.

"Luckily, I was considered pretty and I've always been a little top heavy." A sardonic smile crossed her face for a split second. "So I was able to get a job as an exotic dancer at a nude bar just outside of town. Nobody asked my age and I was makin' enough money to stop hookin' and get my own place. I did that for a while, moved around to more upscale joints over the years once I was legal."

"Is that how you earn a living now?"

"No." She drank more wine. "I eventually got my GED and went to college, stripped at night to pay the bills and the tuition. Just graduated last year." Pride now glowed on Simone's face.

"That's great, honey. I'm really proud of you."

"Me, too. Got a degree in social services. Doesn't pay much, but I think I can help kids who are goin' through hard times like I did. Maybe steer 'em in a better direction."

Mona leaned over and hugged Simone firmly. "You are so strong. I wish I was more like you."

"You've gotta be jokin'!" Simone spread her arms wide and looked around. "Anyone would kill for this house! You've got a fountain in the front yard for Pete's sake! Know what? I wish I were more like you!"

"I've had an easy life for the most part. A challenging marriage, but a life of luxury. So when I hear your story, I realize that my life has been too easy. I'm not strong, resilient, or resourceful. I don't think I could've taken care of myself like you did if I had been in your shoes. I probably would have just killed myself."

"No you wouldn't. Your first reaction when I told you about Clarence was that you woulda killed him! And I believe you."

"That's just talk, just words that anyone could say. Look at you. So pretty, so determined, a survivor. You are my role model."

"I've definitely never thought of myself as a role model, but I appreciate the compliment."

"You're going to be great with those kids. They're going to love you. I just know it."

"I hope you're right. I think I'll be good at it." She smiled. "I haven't landed a job yet, though. I wanted to spend time with you before I accepted a position anywhere."

"Do you have offers?"

"Well, I did graduate at the top of my class so..." Pride lit up her face again.

"That's so wonderful."

"And it would all be shot to hell if it weren't for you." She touched Mona's arm. "Thanks for helpin' me out with the police. I lied when I said I was ready to pay for my past."

"Don't thank me. You shouldn't have to go through more misery. I feel like we let you down, me and Mama."

"No, you didn't let me down, but Beatrice definitely did. That's when she stopped bein' my mama as far as I'm concerned."

They were silent for a few moments as Mona continued smoking her cigarette and Simone drank her wine.

"Anyway, enough about me. The past is the past and I do my best not to think about it. We need to talk about tomorrow and the next day."

Mona blew smoke into the air above her head and watched the mist disperse in the overhead light. "Obviously, we can't stay here. Aaron will probably be out on bail by tomorrow night and I'm sure he'll be upset to find his traitorous wife and her sister sleeping in his house."

"His house?"

"He owns it outright. My name isn't on the deed since he bought it before we were married. But that's not the point. Aaron will not hesitate to beat me senseless once he knows that I'm testifying against him. He wouldn't kill me, of course, but he would certainly want to. So, you see, I can't be here when he gets home."

"I see all too well." Simone narrowed her eyes and nodded her head. "I was married a while back to a sonuvabitch who used to beat my ass if there was no dinner on the table when he got home. I put up with that for around three months before I got tired enough to leave. Thought about killin' him, but then I decided not to test my luck twice in one lifetime. I let him live and just got a divorce."

Mona threw her head back and laughed, soon after being joined by Simone. "He didn't realize who he was dealing with! And now I know how your last name became Edwards." She again blew smoke above her head. "Once again, you've illustrated one of the biggest differences between us. You're so strong, Simone. You decide you don't like something and do something about it. You don't wait for anyone to help you or rescue you. You rescue yourself. I've never been like that, so self-sufficient."

"Well, maybe that's true, but not for long because you're certainly about to move out and stand on your own two feet now."

"And I'm scared to death." Mona struggled against tears, quickly inhaling more nicotine.

"Don't be because we'll get through this together. The first step will be gettin' you and Sophie packed tomorrow morning. I can pack Sophie's stuff while you're visitin' Aaron at the jail."

"That would be very helpful. Thanks."

"Have you thought about where we're goin'?"

"We're getting a room at the Renaissance Hotel downtown. It's very busy, well secured."

"Meanin' that you're already worried about someone tryin' to kill you so you want a lot of people around."

She stubbed out her cigarette. "The idea did cross my mind, yes. Assuming that the police are right about Aaron, that is. I just want to be cautious and make sure my daughter is safe."

"Then maybe we should leave the city altogether. We could even leave Texas for a while until the trial."

"I can't leave Texas. And neither can you. That's part of the deal with the police." Mona's head dropped slightly. "I don't think that I'll be able to satisfy them. They want me to find money that may not even exist."

"So what happens if you never find it? I mean, what if you do everything you can think of to help them, but they're seein' smoke where there's no fire?"

"I don't know. They're hell-bent on the idea that they're right and that I know more than I realize." She exhaled a long, discouraged breath. "All I know is that if there are any bank statements to be found, they're in this house somewhere. Aaron is a control freak and would want to keep anything like that close to him."

"Then let's look for 'em tonight. Maybe we'll get lucky."

"We can look for them, but I doubt that we'll get lucky so quickly, if ever."

"Mommy! Where is my green nightgown?" Sophie was standing at the top of the stairwell with her head poked around a wall.

"It's in your dresser drawer, sweetheart, where it always is."

"I can't find it."

"Then put on the yellow one."

"No! I want the green one!"

Mona looked at Simone and stood up. "I need to put her to bed."

"Okay. While you do that, I'll test my luck and start looking around the place. You can help me once she's asleep."

"Okay. You might want to start in his office. It's just around the corner by the patio doors." Mona went upstairs to find her daughter's favorite gown, her thoughts immersed in the question of whether the police were completely wrong about Aaron. And if they were, would they ever admit it after going to so much trouble to nail him? Probably not. Simone had raised a very valid question: What would happen to her, to all of them, if the police were wrong? Equally as terrifying, what would happen to them if the police were right?

Mona thought about the life her sister had been forced to endure. Most people would have been crushed by so much misery being piled on top of them, but Simone had chosen to survive, to fight back. Tonight Simone had discussed her tragic history with spirit, not dejection, with grief, but not grave depression. How? How had she become so formidable, recognizing her victimization as a child, but rising from the fire a conqueror, a phoenix? Once again, Mona wished that she possessed the relentless strength that Simone had proven to have for most of her life. In the face of so much uncertainty and fear, she could've made good use of even one ounce of it right now.

—✺—

"So, other than his office and his bedroom, where does Aaron spend a lot of his time?" Simone and Mona were standing near his home office the following morning, having had absolutely no luck locating any suspicious bank statements the previous night.

"Uh, he likes to sit outside by the pool."

"Okay, is there anywhere he could stash somethin' out there?"

"No, not really. Nothing comes to mind anyway." They walked to the patio doors and stood looking through the windows at the pool area. There was a very colorful patio table with the standard umbrella above it along with patio chairs.

"You guys actually have a sofa outside! Jees."

"Most people do, I thought."

"No, most people don't, thank you. Remember where you came from." Simone opened one of the patio French doors and walked outside. The September air was stagnant and muggy.

"I'm going to take Sophie to school now and then go to the jail. I should be back in a few hours." Mona was wearing peach silk slacks with a matching blouse, a pearl necklace, and heels. Being well-dressed gave her a sense of power.

"Alright. I'll just keep lookin' around while you're gone." Simone stared at the various flowerbeds surrounding the pool before kicking the dirt around in one of them.

"What are you doing?" Mona was still watching from the open door.

"I just wondered if Aaron had buried the bank statements in one of the flowerbeds. What do you think?"

"I think not. He would never want the dirt under his fingernails. He's fanatical about that sort of thing."

"Oh, okay. You can go on. I'll call ya on your cell if I find anything before ya get back."

Mona just shook her head, knowing full well that nothing would be located. "Be back soon." She went to the kitchen dining table where Sophie was picking at the remaining scrambled eggs on her plate. "What's wrong, honey?"

"I'm full. I don't want anymore."

"That's fine. You probably had too many doughnuts yesterday." She picked up Sophie's plate and walked to the kitchen sink. "Go get your backpack so we can leave."

"Okay." She leapt from the table and ran to her bedroom upstairs, returning shortly out of breath. "Ready!"

"Let's go." They exited the house, got into Mona's black Mercedes sedan, and drove toward Sophie's school. All the while, Mona was rehearsing the best possible way to prepare Sophie for their afternoon relocation to the Renaissance Hotel. "Honey, you and Mommy are going to take a little vacation with Aunt Simone starting today when you're out of school."

"What kind of vacation? Oh! Are we going to Six Flags?"

Mona smiled. "No, sweetie. Not that kind of vacation. We're going to stay in a really nice hotel downtown. You'll get to meet a lot of new people and we'll have a really big room with room service. And, hey! Maybe we'll go get you that President Barbie doll that you've been wanting, too! Doesn't that sound exciting?"

"Is Daddy coming with us?"

"Well, no, honey, Daddy can't come. Daddy and Mommy aren't getting along very well right now. Sometimes Daddies and Mommies have to spend a little time apart so they can work out their differences." Mona held Sophie's eyes for as long as she dared before returning her attention to the traffic around her.

"Are you getting a divorce?"

Mona thought a few long seconds about whether to answer the question. In the end, she decided to be honest with her daughter. "We might, sweetie. Would you be upset with Mommy if that happened?"

Now it was Sophie's turn to be silent as Mona's eyes darted worriedly between her daughter and the road. "Angela said that her parents got divorced when she was a little baby."

"Oh really?" Angela was one of Sophie's friends at school. "How does Angela feel about that?"

Sophie shrugged and puckered her lips. "She said that it's okay."

Since Sophie had changed the subject, Mona wasn't sure how to proceed.

"Mommy, why do you and Daddy have different beds? Julie says that her parents always sleep in the same bed every night."

Julie was another schoolgirl friend. "I guess that Daddy and Mommy were hoping that we could work out our differences that way, honey."

"Julie also says that her Daddy comes home every day."

"That's good."

"But my daddy doesn't come home every day."

Mona faced the road and nodded with tight lips.

"Why doesn't Daddy come home?"

"Because Daddy is very busy with his job and making sure that you are well taken care of."

"But Julie's daddy is busy, too."

Again, Mona nodded silently.

"Mommy?"

"Yes, sweetie."

"Do you think that Daddy loves us?"

"Why would you ask that? Of course Daddy loves us! And he especially loves you very much."

"But I never see him. Angela's daddy takes her to the zoo and he bought her her very own puppy. Daddy never does things like that."

"Have you ever told Daddy how you feel?"

"No."

"Why not?"

To this, Sophie shrugged again and then looked out the car window. They were rounding the corner of her school so Mona slowed to a stop to let her daughter out at the entrance. She paused and stroked Sophie's hair. "Wanna talk some more when I pick you up this afternoon?"

Sophie's response was another shrug as she opened the car door. Before getting out of the car, she leaned toward Mona to receive her daily goodbye kiss, which was promptly planted on her nose.

"Have a good day, baby. I'll be here to get you at 3:30 sharp."

"Okay." She got out of the car and ran toward a group of friends who were walking into the school.

As Mona drove away, tears fell from her eyes, one of the rare moments that she fully succumbed to her emotions. The innocent childhood that she had wanted for Sophie was obviously not going to happen. To Mona's dismay, not only had the child ably rationalized that her parents' marriage was a long way from being ideal, but she had also decided that Aaron didn't love her due to his negligence. And Mona had no one to blame but herself. She had thought that she was doing the right thing for Sophie by providing a two-parent household, but the truth had always been that Mona functioned more like a single parent. Fine with Mona, of course, but not healthy for Sophie to witness every day. Mona had to face the fact that her daughter had been paying an extraordinarily unfair price for Mona's choices, which had been largely based on her resolve to never be poor again. Only now did Mona realize that the illusion of a happy home had been completely obliterated for Sophie a long time ago, before this morning's conversation.

She searched her memory for clues about Sophie's growing awareness of Aaron's coldness, but her memories were limited to the doting that Mona had consistently showered on her daughter, naively thinking that it compensated for Aaron's shortcomings as a father. It seemed that Mona had been naïve about many things that were happening around her. And maybe this lent credence to the police's assumption that she had ignored important signs about Aaron's supposed criminal life. Maybe she hadn't noticed anything suspicious because she hadn't wanted to. Just as she had not noticed that Sophie had begun to question Aaron's love for her. Maybe.

THREE

Still unsettled by the conversation with Sophie, Mona unhappily strode down a sidewalk near the downtown Houston area. Before long, she would be at the Harris County Jail where Aaron was being held and she dreaded seeing him. Once upon a time, he had been the proverbial knight in shining armor when they had met and married, but that knight had long ago vanished, being replaced with someone who required very little cause to become enraged. Years ago, she had tried to patiently inquire into whatever might be bothering him, but had never gotten a straight answer. After a few futile attempts, she had decided to ignore Aaron's moodiness since the most important thing was that she and Sophie wanted for nothing. And that decision might prove to be the worst and most pivotal she had ever made.

As Mona continued toward the jailhouse, she happened to catch a glimpse of her reflection in a Subway sandwich shop window and immediately grimaced at the image that she saw. To her chagrin, the humidity outside had caused her hair to start frizzing, which she viewed as an outward manifestation of the control she was fast losing over everything great and small. And even though her hair didn't look all that bad, her mind's eye saw an exaggerated version that resembled a haphazard bird's nest.

With her agitation quickly escalating, she stopped short and dug into her purse for a hair clip that she could use to pull her hair back. When she looked back up, she noticed another reflection in the window. A man wearing a baseball cap seemed to be watching her from across the street. He was very still, looking straight at her with his hands stuffed in the pockets of his jacket. Why was he wearing a jacket in such humid heat? Her heartbeat instantly quickened as fear replaced her vain discomposure and clogged her throat and stomach. For the first time, she realized exactly how terrified she was by both Richard's and the police's warnings.

Mona didn't have the nerve to turn around and make eye contact with the unknown onlooker. Instead, she hastily resumed walking, almost jogging to the jailhouse, which was one block away and within sight. From where she was, she could already see a handful of policemen entering and exiting the building and she had never been so glad to see their blue uniforms in her life.

—⁂—

By the time Aaron ambled into the jailhouse meeting room, Mona, who was still combatting acute edginess, had been seated and staring into space for over ten minutes. Wearing a baggy orange prisoner jumpsuit, he looked deceptively skinny, but he was actually quite lean, muscular, and exceptionally good looking in an unusual way. His teeth weren't perfectly straight, but his smile was nevertheless infectious. Olive-toned skin, dark curly hair that was normally tamed with expensive gels, very ordinary facial features and an average height of 5'10". At age thirty-five, his unfailing confidence was his most winning and, to women, sexiest attribute, promoting his everyday looks to something more along the lines of profound. And, as Mona knew well, he was very good in bed. That always helped. But to see his true essence, it was incumbent on the beholder that Aaron's eyes receive particular attention. They were black pearls, emotionless, shiny like a snake's when stalking prey and waiting to strike. Although the danger was evident in his eyes, Mona had not been looking for it when they met years ago. She had been concerned with only one bottom line: his money. He was an opportunity to live a better life than what she had known by then at age nineteen.

Now at the jailhouse, he swaggered, his confident air unabated by the handcuffs. As far as Mona could see, he was in no way daunted by his surroundings or the policeman gripping his arm as they walked toward the table. Aaron impassively looked at Mona as they crossed the room, his eyes never leaving hers even when he was practically shoved down into the chair across the table from her. He half-smirked as she nervously watched him, neither of them speaking until the officer had stepped away from them.

Mona kept her hands in her lap and her back against her chair, ensuring that no portion of her body was within reach of Aaron. He would literally have to jump across the table to get to her, but she was still nervous. "Hello, Aaron. Are you doing okay?" Her voice quivered, which was stupid because she knew she was safe.

Aaron didn't reply. He merely continued with his unwavering stare and the cocky smirk.

"Aaron? I said how are you?" Mona confusedly looked from him to the police officer standing a few feet away. "Aaron?"

The door was flung open and a short, stout, gray-haired man walked in wearing an expensive gray suit and carrying a briefcase. "I apologize for being a little late, Mr. and Mrs. Baker. Rush hour traffic was slower than a hung jury." He pulled a chair out from the table while also obtaining spectacles from his coat pocket. "Get it? Hung jury? They talk and talk for days." As he sat down, he met Mona's bewildered expression and Aaron's unappreciative smile. "Bad joke. Sorry. Anyway, I'm here now. What have I missed?"

"I'm sorry..." Mona began before being cut short by Aaron.

"You haven't missed anything, Tom. I was waiting for you to get here." He and Tom shook hands as the police officer left the room.

"Ah, good!"

"What is this about?" Mona looked at Aaron and gestured to Tom. "Who is he and why is he here?"

"My name is Tom Cedar and I'm Aaron's defense attorney. I'm here, Mrs. Baker, to make sure that my client's rights are protected. It is our understanding that you have brokered a deal with the police to testify against your husband in exchange for certain immunities for your recently located sister. Because you have made this agreement, anything that my client says today could be used against him in court should the case reach that point. Therefore, my client has requested my presence." Despite the awkward circumstances of his attendance, Tom was poised and even jovial. "Now, Mrs. Baker, your husband may not be at liberty to speak with you about some topics that may be on your mind this morning. If you ask any questions that I believe are counterproductive to his defense, I will instruct him to remain silent, at which time you may proceed to another unrelated matter. Is this clear?"

Throughout Tom's explanation, Mona's mystified gaze flitted between Tom and Aaron. "Y-yes, I understand, but is this really necessary?"

"I'm afraid it is, Mrs. Baker. Now, pretend that I'm not here, if you like. Just keep your questions limited to matters that don't pertain to the case."

Aaron was smug as he stared at Mona from across the table. An ominous pause hung between them before, "So, little wife, why did you want to see me? What could you possibly want?" The sarcasm in his voice made Mona's already delicate stomach wrench. She swallowed dryly.

"I-I came to tell you about, uh...well, I –"
"Yes?"
"I-I was going to tell you about the police. I thought I owed you that much." She could barely meet his eyes.

"Oh really?"

"Yes, but you've already heard so…"

"That's right. I've heard about your heartless betrayal, which, I might add, doesn't surprise me. So be it. What else?"

After a short pause, Mona continued in a strained voice. "I also thought you'd like to know that your daughter and I are moving out of the house today. We won't be there when you get home."

He snorted. "My daughter?" He rolled his eyes toward the ceiling. "That's right, my supposed daughter. Well, now there's a little story that I'm going to share with you. Shoulda told you a long time ago, but, see, I used to actually love you and I didn't think you'd marry a guy who couldn't give you children."

Mona's eyes widened with surprise, but she remained silent.

"That's right, Mona. I can't have any kids of my own because I'm sterile, a fact I've known since I went to college and tried to donate sperm for a little extra cash. Found out that I don't have any swimmers. No swimmers, no moolah." He rubbed his fingers together. "So imagine my surprise when you come tell me that you're pregnant a few months after we're married. What's a guy to think? Did my sperm defy every medical expert who confirmed my infertile lot in life? Or," he leaned forward as Mona reflexively shrank backward, "has the little woman been screwing around? And so soon after we'd tied the knot, no less." He leaned backward to rest his back against his chair again. "It would seem that there is no such thing as a trustworthy woman, even when a man takes her from squalor and gives her the world as I did for you."

"You are hardly one to cast stones, Aaron." Some small amount of resentment now found its way into Mona's voice. "I know about all your women. People talk and you certainly haven't cared to be discreet."

"Yes, Mona, you're right. I've been unfaithful, but not until you told me you were pregnant." Black pearl eyes.

To this response, Mona could only cast her eyes to the table, feeling shame for her infidelity for the first time since marrying Aaron. She thought about lighting a cigarette, but remembered that smoking wasn't allowed.

"So if you want to move out and take your bitch daughter with you, I say good riddance and perfect timing. Get out and don't even think about trying to come back."

Unexpectedly taken aback, Mona closed her eyes and briefly recalled the early months of their marriage. Aaron had been good to her, but she had never been in love with him. And she had assumed that he – as with all men in her estimation – was incapable of being loyal to her. Therefore, she consciously avoided investing or even contemplating any serious emotions for Aaron. She remembered the amazement, not happiness, on his face when she had told him of her pregnancy, expecting him to celebrate the news. Instead of rejoicing, however, he had left the house, returning in a drunken stupor late that night with no explanation. Things between them had not been the same afterward, but Mona had been too consumed with her personal greed to care. Now it all made sense. He had always known that Sophie wasn't his daughter and he had lived with that truth every day for nearly eight years, hating the sight of the child, and out of that hatred beating Mona for bearing living proof of her treachery.

"I'm sorry for what I've done, Aaron." She looked at the table before raising her eyes to meet his. "You were good to me once, but I'm not the only one of us at fault here. You never told me the truth about how you were making your money."

"Mrs. Baker, I'm afraid I'll need to stop you there and ask you to discuss something else," Tom quickly interjected.

"You never told me that you were trafficking drugs, Aaron!" Mona was nearly yelling now with angry defiance. "That everything I knew about you was just one big lie!"

"Mrs. Baker, please!"

"No, it's okay, Tom."

"Aaron, I'm going to insist that you remain silent."

"I understand your advice, counselor, and I am choosing to ignore it." Aaron's eyes slowly slid from Tom to Mona. "I'm curious to know exactly what about your life with me has been a lie, Mona? I mean, other than the birth of your illegitimate child, who you've tried to pass off as mine for over seven years." He paused deliberately. "You've been to my office at work so you know I have a high-ranking job. You've been to a number of parties with my business associates present. I'm sure that the police have already told you that my bank account is squeaky clean. So what have I lied about?"

"What about the drugs, Aaron?" Mona's voice trembled with fear and anger. "How do you explain the drugs at the house?"

"Why, they were planted there, of course." He laughed haughtily and looked at Tom.

"That's enough, Aaron. As your attorney –"

"Do you really think that I would be so stupid as to store cocaine in my own home? If I were moving it between cities, that is, as the police have charged. Really, give me a break."

"Who would want to plant drugs in the house?" Mona's tone was incredulous.

"I don't know! But that's what the police need to go investigate instead of trying to get me to admit to something I haven't done!"

Mona pondered the validity of Aaron's statements for a few moments before shaking her head with disbelief.

"Once again, Aaron, I must insist that you –"

"What? You don't believe me? Well, just wait for the trial if there is one. The truth will come out."

"You're pathetic, you know that?" Mona pushed her chair back and stood up, grabbing her purse from the floor.

"May I remind you, dear wife, that you are in no position to judge anyone. You're nothing but a tramp, a bloodsucking gold digger who trades her body for a house, clothes, and a car. I should have put you out the day you said you were pregnant because you certainly haven't earned your keep since then." The contempt in his voice and eyes was palpable.

"Then why didn't you? Huh?" Now Mona was seething, an emotional state that usually led to their physical clashes at home as Mona's embattled pride rebelled against the reigns of perpetual denial while Aaron's damaged ego demanded satisfaction. "Why didn't you put me out? Because you'd rather keep me around as an occasional punching bag whenever you decided to come home? To punish me for having Sophie?"

"I let you stay because I loathed the idea of all my friends and relatives finding out that they had been right about you. And it was easier than suffering the humiliation of having your wanton acts publicized. I would have looked like a fool, you see." He smugly watched Mona, who was still standing on the other side of the table. "But lately, I have to say I've wished that you would just drop dead because my life would be so much easier. And who knows? People die every day. My luck may change soon enough."

That was it. Mona clenched her purse strap and started walking around the table. Before passing Aaron, she stopped, hocked saliva, and spit into his face. "You bastard. Let me assure you that I intend to live a long, long time." She walked toward the door and called over her shoulder, "I'll see you in court."

—◦◦◦—

Once again seated in her Mercedes and heading home, Mona could hardly concentrate on driving. A substantial amount of her anger toward Aaron had given way to nervous fear as she kept visualizing his arrogance and hearing his last comment about her dying. Had that been a threat? If so, she probably couldn't prove it. Still, she thought it was a good idea to bring it to Harold's attention. With her eyes facing forward on the road, Mona grabbed her cell phone from her purse and flipped the top open. Before she could start dialing, however, the phone began to ring. She glanced at the caller ID screen and saw that it was Jocelyn, her most recent extra-marital escapade. A few years ago, Mona had discovered that women and men could be used interchangeably depending upon her mood. Men were good for random romps in the hay, which was often good enough for Mona. Women, on the other hand, helped her to release all her stress through both physical and verbal connections, intimacies that women naturally craved all at once as opposed to enduring one without the other as they so often did in their relationships with men. But while Mona enjoyed the experience of feeling needed for more than just her body, she was not interested in reciprocating such an emotion so she had to be more careful with the women.

She pressed a button on the phone to answer the call. "Hi, Jocelyn. You've caught me at a bad time." Mona's hurried indifference was apparent in her voice.

"Hey, babe." Jocelyn's throaty voice contained relief and excitement. "I've been worried about you since I hadn't heard from you lately."

"Yeah, well, I've been busy. My husband was arrested yesterday and it's been a nightmare ever since."

"Oh my god! What happened?"

"Long story. Listen, I gotta go. I was just about to call one of the detectives when my phone rang. Don't worry." She ended the call without waiting for Jocelyn's response and then called information. "Can I please get the phone number for the police department in Harris County?" The phone number was soon being repeated by a recorded voice. Mona selected the option to have her call automatically connected to the police station and then asked for Harold. To her disappointment, she was put through to his voice mail and so left a message requesting that he call her back as soon as possible. His business card was on her kitchen counter at home so she could try his cell phone later if she didn't hear from him within a couple of hours.

Mona soon turned into her driveway and shut off the car engine. Before she could even open the car door, Simone appeared near the front fender. "How'd it go, girl?" She approached the car and closed the door for Mona after she had gotten out.

"Terrible. I don't know what I ever saw in him." They walked into the house together. "How about you? Did you manage to find anything?"

"No, but I got plenty of Sophie's clothes packed. I also made some lunch in case you're hungry."

"Thanks, but I don't have an appetite." Now they were climbing the stairwell so Mona could begin packing for herself. "You know, I think that Aaron actually threatened me with his attorney sitting right beside him."

"You can't be serious."

"Yes, he said something about me dropping dead so that his life would be easier."

"Do you think he meant it?"

"I don't know, but I've left a message for Harold to call me."

"What do ya think he can do?" Simone immediately sounded wary.

"He probably can't do anything, but at least he'll know that Aaron may be planning something. And there was also some weird guy on the street that –" The phone rang so Mona hastened her steps, reaching the phone in her bedroom on the fourth ring. "Hello?"

"Mrs. Baker? It's Harold. I got your message. Is everything alright?"

"Harold! Thank God." She was genuinely grateful to receive the call so quickly. "I just saw Aaron at the jail a short time ago and I think he threatened my life." She recounted what Aaron had said verbatim as Harold listened without interruption.

"You have nothing to worry about. We've been concerned that your husband may try to flee the country before the trial so we're keeping him under surveillance when he's bailed out today. He can't come near you without us knowing it." He sounded very confident, which gave Mona some measure of comfort. "Your attorney has informed us that you and your sister are relocating to the Renaissance Hotel today. Is that correct?"

"Yes, that's right."

"Okay, then I'll need to get your room number when you check in so we can reach you there. We're also going to post an officer outside your door so you have some protection."

"But you just said that Aaron can't get near me." Mona had rapidly shifted to feeling alarmed for Sophie's safety.

"And that's true, but he could hire someone else to do his dirty work."

Mona's breath choked at hearing Harold speak her own thoughts.

"Mrs. Baker?"

"I-I'm alright," she stammered. "It's just that I saw some guy staring at me on the street this morning when I was on my way to see Aaron. It's probably nothing."

"That's all the more reason for us to assign protection to you. Maybe that guy was a passing admirer, but maybe not. He could've been a warning to let you know that you're being watched. And that's just for starters."

Mona was on the verge of outright panic as she weighed both Harold's warning and his offer of police protection. But her decision wasn't as simple as he seemed to think it should be. Despite his apparent good intentions, she had trouble believing that the police would do everything possible to keep her safe if Aaron actually wanted her dead. One of his closest friends was the mayor, a man with power over the police. And she had to consider the possibility that Aaron's potential guilt implicated the mayor along with any number of policemen as well. "I'm sorry, Harold, but I just can't put our lives in your department's hands. My husband has friends everywhere and I'm certain that some of those friends are cops that you trust." Her hand trembled as she held the phone to her ear. "You should have seen the look on his face when I saw him this morning. He's not worried about any of you."

"I think you're making a big mistake, Mrs. Baker. We know the types of people that your husband is working for and these guys don't play around."

Mona's eyes drifted to Simone, who was standing beside her and watching her face. "What did he say?"

Mona merely shook her head as she thought about Harold's statements. Images of Sophie being stabbed, shot, or choked cluttered her mind. "Okay, Harold, okay. I'll call you with our room number once we get checked in."

"I'm sending someone to your house to follow you to the hotel."

"I'd prefer that you not do that. I'll call you with the room number like I said." She heard Harold sigh as though exasperated.

"Very well, Mrs. Baker. An officer will be there before your husband is released."

"And when do you think that might be?"

"I'm not sure. This evening, maybe around six o'clock."

"Okay." Mona was breathless, but hopeful that she had just made the right decision. "Thank you, Harold."

When she hung up the phone, Simone pounced with questions. "What's goin' on? Why does he need our room number?"

"So he can reach me if he needs to." She stood silently, distracted with her thoughts.

"And? I got the impression that there's more to it."

"He's going to have an officer stationed outside our door at the hotel to make sure we're safe." Mona hurriedly started toward her closet.

"Protection? Police are worse than the criminals on the street! They take payoffs, they steal from the crooks they're arresting, they set up people, they rape prostitutes, they plant evidence –"

"Okay! I get it!" Mona began flinging various clothes from her closet onto her bed, taking whatever was next on the racks without bothering to see what did or didn't match. It was already 1:00 PM and she needed to get checked in and unpacked at the hotel before picking up Sophie from school. "Look, what do you want me do? I have a daughter to think about. Believe me, I wish we didn't need the police to protect us because Aaron is cozy with 'em, I'm sure. But I don't see what choice I have right now." She threw her suitcases onto the bed and began unloading her underwear into one of them as she continued talking. "If you've got some bright ideas, I'm listening."

"There's just gotta be another way. I'm tellin' ya, cops are bad news."

"Well, maybe we'll get lucky. I don't know. We'll put a chair against the door to make sure no one gets in, not even the cop guarding us. How's that?" It was a weak attempt to reduce the mounting tension they both felt. It didn't work.

"Yeah, sure." Simone's tone was rife with disgust. "What about money? And I need to get clothes from my place."

"Don't worry about money. I've been squirreling away cash for years." She sat on top of one of the suitcases so she could close and lock it. "Plus, I nearly emptied out the bank account this morning before going to the jail. We'll be fine." Since the police had failed to connect Aaron's known bank account to any illicit activities, Mona had been able to access the funds.

"Okay."

"Where do you live?"

"In League City."

"Fine. We'll go to your place tomorrow after I drop Sophie off at school." Mona placed her three bursting suitcases on the floor. "Will you help me carry these to the car?"

"Okay." Simone proceeded to grab two suitcases, but after attempting to lift one, she had to set the other one back down. "Feels like you've got bricks in here." She used both of her hands to lift the heavier suitcase and waddled from the room. Mona followed behind with the clothes remaining on hangers loaded into her arms. When she reached the doorway, she turned and looked back at her bedroom. It was very likely that she would never see this room again after today and she was both distressed and saddened. Her life was about to change forever and she had no idea whether or not she was leaping from the frying pan into the fire.

FOUR

"Good evening, Mrs. Baker. I'm Officer Frank Costello and the department has assigned me to guard you and your family every evening for as long as necessary." He was standing in the doorway of Mona's elegant two-bedroom Renaissance Hotel room with his identification held out for her to inspect. Frank looked to be in his early twenties and had dark features, his hair hidden neatly beneath his black police uniform hat.

It was around 7:00 PM and Mona had been eating dinner with Sophie and Simone when they'd heard the knock at their door. Upon seeing the officer, she logically assumed that Aaron would soon be released. Mona crossed her arms in a reflexive posture of agitation. "Hello, Officer Costello. Thank you for coming and helping us. May I offer you anything? Something to drink perhaps?" He didn't look intimidating to her so he probably wouldn't scare off anyone seeking to harm her or Sophie. She could only hope that his appearance was deceiving and that he wasn't wet behind the ears.

"No, ma'am. I've secured a chair from the hotel management and I have a newspaper. That's all I need. I just wanted to introduce myself and let you know that I'm here."

"Thank you."

"Also, my duty is scheduled for the evenings. Tomorrow morning, Officer Abbey Sebastian will be posted for your protection and then Officer Stanley Zanowich in the afternoon."

"Okay, thank you for letting me know."

"It's no problem, ma'am." He bent forward slightly and then turned toward his chair, which was positioned immediately to the left of the door.

Mona closed the door not knowing if she felt safer or more worried. She and her family were being guarded by a police officer who looked more like a college student.

"Who was that?" Simone asked between bites of her grilled fish as Mona walked back into the living room where Simone and Sophie were still eating in front of the television.

"That was Officer Costello letting us know that he'll be posted outside our door to protect us."

"The policeman is here?" Sophie's voice was full of wonder and awe. She didn't fully understand why the officer was ordered to guard them, but she had known that he would be arriving.

"That's right, sweetheart."

"Can I meet him? Please, please, pretty please?" She was already standing up, prepared to abandon her own dinner of fried chicken.

"Not until you finish your dinner so sit back down and make sure you clean your plate."

"Oh, okay." Disappointed, Sophie plopped back down onto her chair, her two ponytails swinging aimlessly beside her head.

Mona couldn't hide the smile that spread across her face as she observed her little girl. Sophie seemed to be adjusting very quickly to their new quarters. It helped to have Simone here lavishing extra attention on Sophie, who was happily bonding with her aunt. "I think I'll take a shower now."

"Go ahead. I'll watch Sophie."

"Thanks." Mona went into the spacious bedroom that she and Sophie would share for an indefinite amount of time. Could be weeks, could be months. Most of their clothes had been unpacked and the covers on the king-size bed were turned down. As Mona went into the bathroom, she wondered where Aaron was and what he might be doing.

—⁓—

Mona hardly slept that night as she listened to Sophie's soft, rhythmic breathing beside her in bed. Her daughter was blissfully unaware of the danger that they might be facing, which was as it should be as far as Mona was concerned. She loved her little girl more than anything or anyone and she was determined to shoulder whatever horrors might lie ahead, the thoughts of which prevented her from even a fitful slumber that night. When Mona emerged from her bedroom the following morning, she was more exhausted than when she had gone to bed. But her weariness was immediately usurped by her surprise at finding Simone blanketed and asleep in an armchair facing the door instead of in her own room. "Simone?" She lightly shook her sister until she awoke. "What are you doing out here? Did you sleep in this chair last night?"

Simone shifted in the chair, groggy with sleep. "Yeah."

"Why?" Mona was whispering to ensure she didn't wake Sophie.

"So I could watch the door and make sure no one tried to get in." Simone sat up and stretched her arms in the air, slowly coming fully awake.

"But you knew that Frank would be stationed outside our room all night."

"I already told ya that I don't trust cops."

"Frank is harmless. You met him."

"There's no such thing as a harmless cop."

"Okay, fine." Mona gave up and walked to a phone to order breakfast. "I'm not going to debate with you about it."

Simone stood up and began walking toward her bedroom with the blanket from her bed. "There's nothing to debate about. If you'd seen what I've seen, you'd understand what I'm sayin'."

"But Frank almost looks like a kid."

"Trust none of 'em, Mona. I don't care how they look." She disappeared into her room and closed the door.

—✍—

Later that morning, the sisters entered Simone's tiny studio apartment in League City to collect some of her clothes and toiletries. Altogether, the apartment was around 550 square feet, a solitary room with only two doors, one for the bathroom entry and the other for a single closet. Aside from a bowl of uneaten cereal on the kitchen counter, everything was very tidy and in its place.

Mona was aghast at how differently she and Simone had been living. Hearing about Simone's harsh history of financial deprivation was one thing, but seeing the evidence of it was another thing entirely. In fact, it was depressing. Simone's apartment was smaller than Mona's bathroom, an appalling way to live, she thought to herself. But Simone seemed to be proud of her apartment.

"So what do ya think? Pretty cool, huh? I mean, not much compared to your place, but I like it."

Mona couldn't think of anything remotely pleasant to say other than, "It's very clean."

Simone looked at Mona's strained face and laughed. "Girl, you really have gotten a stick up your ass since you married Aaron! You've lost touch with your roots." She walked over to her closet and opened the door as Mona remained motionless in the center of the room, still struggling to come to grips with her sister's miniature home. "How'd ya meet him anyway?"

Mona finally walked to a small sofa, sat down, and immediately began fishing for a cigarette in her purse. "We met at the library when I was nineteen."

"The library? What were you doin' at the library? You don't even like to read." Simone was filling a duffle bag with clothes as she spoke.

"I like to read okay." She tapped a cigarette out of the package and lit it, soon inhaling deeply.

"Yeah, right."

"I do. Enough anyway, I guess."

"Alright, so y'all met at the library and then what?"

"He noticed that I was looking at SAT books and offered to help me study. I thought it was a little obvious, but sweet."

"And so you fell in love with him."

"No." Mona looked around for an ashtray in vain. "Got any ashtrays?"

"No, I don't smoke."

"So what can I use then?"

"Just use a coffee mug. They're in the cabinet left of the kitchen sink." Simone stuffed socks and t-shirts into a duffle bag as she talked. "I don't have to tell ya that smokin' might kill ya."

"Lots of things can kill any one of us at any time." Mona located a mug, tapped the cigarette on the edge to discard the white ashes, and quickly took another drag.

"Yeah, I guess you've got bigger problems than a cancer stick right now. Your husband might like to kill ya long before that cigarette will."

"Maybe." She exhaled a stream of smoke and watched Simone efficiently packing various pairs of pants, folding them neatly and placing them in the only suitcase she appeared to own.

"So why did ya marry a man that you didn't even love?"

"For the same reason that most women marry wealthy men, I guess."

Simone rolled her eyes and shut her suitcase.

"What?" Mona became defensive. "You have a problem?"

"I'm just surprised that you would do somethin' like that since we were raised to take care of ourselves."

"But why should our lives be harder than they have to be? Look at your place here. It's a rat cage! You have almost no furniture or clothes. While you were stripping in nightclubs, I was vacationing on Brazilian beaches or at Martha's Vineyard, living in a mansion with enough money at my fingertips to buy just about anything I could think of. You said yourself that you'd like to be me and to have my life and the more I find out about you, the more I understand why."

Simone picked up her suitcase and held her duffle bag strap to her shoulder. She then walked toward her sister at a deliberately slow pace while responding. "That's right, I said that. And maybe I thought it was true, but I don't feel that way anymore. You've paid a helluva price for your free ride, Mona. Your husband is a drug trafficker who wants you dead, your residential address is now a hotel, and you don't trust anyone enough to have a friend to lean on." Simone stopped in front of Mona as they impudently held each other's eyes. "Obviously, I haven't been livin' in a palace like you or buyin' Gucci purses and Chanel dresses, but ya know what? I've been happy. I've had my own place, bought my own stuff, lived on my own terms, and accepted no bullshit from anyone because I don't have to. You can't say any of that because you've chosen to live like a parasite. You're sad. And I feel sorry for you." Simone gravely held Mona's eyes a few moments longer before stepping around her toward the door as Mona morosely lowered her eyes to the floor.

"You're right. I'm sorry for saying any of that. You're much stronger than I've ever been in my life."

Simone's facial expression softened slightly. "It hasn't been easy, Mona, but it has been worth it to get where I am today. Who and what would I be if I hadn't gone through so much hell? I certainly wouldn't be prepared to deal with your situation without peein' in my pants." She opened the door and turned to look at Mona again. "I also wouldn't have several hundred-thousand dollars in the bank." Mona's jaw dropped with shock. "I'm good at savin'. And you'd be surprised what a good stripper can make." She winked and stepped through the door. "Come on. Let's get outta here."

Dumbfounded, Mona remained motionless for a split second longer before turning to the kitchen sink and running water over her neglected cigarette to extinguish it. She then crossed over to the sofa to grab her purse. "I can't believe that you didn't mention that to me earlier!"

"Why would I?" Simone locked the door and they walked down the stairwell to the parking lot. "I'm gonna follow you back to the hotel in my car."

"You have a car?"

"Of course I have a car!" Simone pressed a button on her key chain, disarming a car alarm on a bluish-gray Jaguar. Again, Mona's jaw dropped when she realized which car belonged to her sister. "It's one of the few treats that I've allowed myself." Simone smiled as she opened the back door and set her suitcase and duffle bag inside.

"Why would you buy a Jaguar and yet live in a matchbox?"

"Girl, I own a beach house in Galveston. I just been rentin' this place to be closer to you until we could work things out." She got into the car, closed the door, and started the engine as Mona stood agape by the car door. Finally, Simone let her window down. "Would ya please go get in your car so we can leave?"

"Yeah, okay." Mona's legs ignored the mental command to move.

"Now!"

"Okay, okay." She turned around and made the short walk to her Mercedes, which was parked a few cars over. Soon afterward, the sisters pulled away from Simone's apartment and turned onto the street that would take them back toward the hotel. Neither of them noticed the white Ford Taurus that vigilantly followed a few cars behind.

—⁊⁊⁊—

After dropping Simone's car and belongings off at the hotel, the sisters headed back out, this time to Aaron's house. They were hoping he wouldn't be home so they could search more rooms for the mysterious bank records. The Renaissance Hotel was only a few miles from River Oaks so it wasn't long before the women were cruising through the neighborhood. Having made the drive countless times, Mona hardly noticed the individual houses anymore, but Simone oohed and ahhed at the multimillion dollar mansions with each turn. Before they reached Aaron's home, Mona's cell phone rang. She fished the phone from her purse and flipped the top to answer the call.

"Hello?"

"What's up, baby?" It was Lyle, another one of Mona's extracurricular activities. This particular affair had run out of gas a few months ago, but Lyle, who owned a Mexican restaurant near the River Oaks subdivision, wasn't ready to give up.

Mona was already sorry that she'd answered the phone. "I thought I told you not to call me anymore." From the corner of her eye, Mona noticed that Simone's interest had abruptly shifted from the scenery to her profile.

"Women always change their minds or say no when they mean yes." His voice reminded Mona of goo, sopping with lustful confidence. It was this quality plus his unceasing neediness that had turned her off after sleeping with him a few times.

"Neither of those stereotypes applies to me."

"Yeah they do. You're just playing hard to get. But I don't mind. It's fun. Makes it more challenging to bag you so I'll play along."

Mona huffed disgustedly and clamped the phone down to end the call. "Pervert."

"Who was that?" Simone's eyebrow arched upward with obvious suspicion.

"Nobody. Just some jerk who doesn't know how to get lost." Mona pulled up to a curb near Aaron's house and stopped to survey the driveway for his car. "Looks like he's at home. Damn!" Her phone rang again. She checked the caller ID screen this time before answering and saw that the call was coming from inside the house. It had to be Aaron. Her first instinct was to let the call roll into voice mail, but she dreaded hearing a recorded message from him equally as much as she hated the idea of talking to him now. Choosing to get it over with, she flipped the top of the phone to answer the call while staring at the front yard of the house.

"What?" Mona's greeting was chilly to say the least.

"You bitch! Where do you get off withdrawing nearly all the money in my bank account?"

"Haven't you heard, Aaron? What's yours is mine."

Upon hearing Aaron's name, Simone's eyes widened as she listened intently.

Aaron chuckled coldly on the line. "Well, not anymore, darlin'. I've opened a new account without your name on it and transferred every dime into it. You've had your last payday at my expense."

"What's the matter? Your drug money won't cover your legal expenses without the cops figuring it out?"

He slammed the phone down in Mona's ear without another word.

"Yep, he's definitely at home." Mona continued to look at the front yard, really seeing it for the first time in several years. That front yard used to be hers. She used to live in the magnificent seven-bedroom house behind it.

"You played that very calmly with Aaron. I'm impressed."

Mona turned to look at Simone with a small, sad smile. "Maybe you're rubbing off on me."

"Or maybe you're rememberin' who you really are."

"Yeah. Maybe." Mona's phone rang yet again.

"Boy you're popular!"

Mona grimaced and glanced at the caller ID, but she didn't recognize the caller's phone number. "Hello?"

"Mrs. Baker, why are you parked across the street from your husband's residence?" It was Harold.

"How do you know where I am?" She started looking around the area beyond her car window.

"Because I'm parked further up on the other side and facing your car. Look up to your right." Mona complied. "See that black Ford Explorer?"

"Yes."

"I'm sitting in it looking straight at you."

Mona turned to Simone and pointed to the Explorer. "Harold is in that car watching us."

"What are you doing here?" He asked again.

"We just wanted to see if Aaron was at home so we could look for those bank records."

"Bad timing for that. He's in there."

"I think his car in the driveway tipped us off to that fact, Detective."

"You're a shrewd sleuth, Mrs. Baker." His tone was playful.

Mona momentarily wondered if he was flirting with her, but the thought quickly passed out of her mind. "We'll just try back in a couple of days. Maybe he'll be working again by then."

"Unless he's fired first. Or put on an indefinite leave of absence. Most employers wouldn't want a company officer accused of illegal drug activities to show up at the office." Harold's voice had resumed the typical dry, humorless quality.

"Oh. I hadn't thought about that."

"Anyway, it's pointless for you to search the house because we've already turned it inside out while we questioned you and your husband the other day. If the records were there, we would have found them."

"Are you sure about that?"

"Positive."

Mona rubbed her chin and looked at Simone, who was clearly dying to know what was being said at the other end of the line. "If you're right about Aaron having a secret account, the proof is in the house. He would want the documents close to him."

"That's a dead horse, Mrs. Baker, but if you're determined to kick it, I won't stop you. Just keep in mind that the bank records are part of our deal."

"What if we never find them?" Mona was getting annoyed with the man.

"Then the deal is off."

Mona exhaled her frustration and stared at Harold's vehicle. She couldn't really see his face, only his silhouette from where she was parked. In that instant, she hated him and the whole police department for so callously using her and Simone. Was their stupid drug case really more important than three innocent people's lives? Of course, the police didn't consider Simone innocent, but Simone had been driven to kill a man who had been molesting her for two years. Surely they understood her frame of mind, the rage that had overwhelmed a teenager who couldn't rely on the legal system to help her without also further damaging her life. She exchanged looks with Simone again, feeling a mixture of anger at the detective and love for her sister at the same time. "Detective, I have a question, if you don't mind."

"Alright."

"I've been trying to figure out how you knew that my sister was at Clarence's apartment the night he was killed."

"Because her prints were all over the place, including his wallet."

"Yeah, yeah. You've told me that and so has Simone. But how did you know that the fingerprints were hers? How did you match them when she's never been arrested before?"

"Easy. Starbucks."

"Excuse me?"

"Starbucks. Your sister bought coffee at Starbucks almost every morning before she drove by your house. One of my men followed her and recovered one of her discarded coffee cups from the trash. That's how we got her prints, but we didn't know at the time they would match the prints at your uncle's apartment. We were just trying to figure out who she was since she kept coming by your house. We got lucky with the match to the crime scene. Took some more legwork to find out who she was, though."

"So why didn't you arrest her?"

"Because, Mrs. Baker, your uncle was a known sex offender, one of the worst kinds of psychos out here and we were all glad when somebody offed him. A couple of other detectives had been investigating him for years due to molestation complaints being filed, but there was never enough evidence to indict him. Or parents would suddenly decide that they didn't want their children put through more trauma with trials. So when he turned up dead, nobody put much effort into finding his killer, although some of us wanted to shake his – or her, as it turns out – hand."

"Why wasn't anyone in my family told about him?"

"Our records show that your mother was questioned a few times. She even provided alibis for him if she thought she could. Never could understand that."

"She never said a word to us about it." Mona's anger was depleted as retrospective sadness crushed her. "If only Simone and I had known." Beside her looking more and more anxious, Simone continued to listen carefully, but was unable to garner much without hearing Harold's comments at the other end of the line.

Harold was silent.

"Detective, you don't really want my sister in prison, do you?"

"The short answer is no. She did the world a service by shooting your uncle. The long answer is that we won't hesitate to put her in prison if you don't keep your end of the bargain. Murder is murder, Mrs. Baker, whether or not we liked the victim."

"God, I hate you."

"I'm just doing my job. It's not personal."

"It is personal! You're risking my family's lives for a stupid drug case that won't even make a difference after everything is said and done!"

"If we can keep the drugs out of the hands of one kid, then we've made a difference."

"Well, what about my kid, huh? What about her? What if she gets killed or I get killed? Is it worth that to you?"

"I have offered to put you in a safe house and you turned me down. Have you changed your mind?"

"How could I find the bank records if I'm in a god-damned safe house?"

"You can either tell us where to look or I can assign two officers to escort you to all destinations of your choosing while your daughter remains at the safe house under protection."

"Leave my daughter with people I can't even trust? Are you kidding me?"

"She would be safe, Mrs. Baker."

"You can't guarantee that."

"Mrs. Baker, be rational. We –"

Mona disconnected the call and remained silent, again enraged as well as discouraged. Meanwhile,

Simone was eager to know everything that had been said.

"Well?"

Mona shifted her car into gear and pulled away from the curb without responding. As she passed the black Explorer in which Harold was sitting, both she and Simone looked into the car, only briefly catching a glimpse of Harold returning their looks through his windshield.

"Come on, what did he say?"

"I'll tell you once I've had a drink." She reached down into her purse and whipped out a pack of cigarettes.

"Oh no! You're not smokin' with me in the car!"

"I'll just hold it between my lips then. But when we get to the bar, I'm smoking the whole pack."

FIVE

The hotel room was dark, deceptively peaceful and quiet as everyone either slept or attempted to sleep. After Mona and Sophie had gone to bed, Simone had promptly retrieved the blanket from her bed and once again prepared a makeshift resting spot on a soft armchair located near a window several hundred square feet away from the main hotel room door that she faced. She wanted to be comfortable, but not so much so that she was likely to sleep deeply, perhaps too soundly to hear an intruder attempting to break in. Tonight, she was even better prepared for a prowler than she had been last night thanks to the Smith and Wesson handgun that now rested in her palm beneath the blanket. Mona had not seen Simone slip the weapon into her duffle bag when they were at her apartment that morning and Simone was pretty sure that Mona would be upset if she knew that a gun had been brought into such close proximity with Sophie. But it was protection, much more reliable than the cop sitting outside their door. And Simone was an excellent shot. Forget karate, kickboxing, and other forms of hand-to-hand self-defense methods. A bullet would drop anyone without the need to break a sweat so Simone had learned to fire various types of hand guns with supreme accuracy, a skill that made her feel much more secure in a world that preyed on helplessness.

She folded her legs beneath the blanket and watched the door for a short time before allowing the heaviness of her eyelids to have their way. Beneath the blanket, she kept her thumb on the gun's safety and her fingers wrapped around the handle. Simone was confident that she could aim, fire, and kill within a matter of seconds if necessary as long as she dozed as lightly as possible. The trick to merely dozing was the odd position she was forced to assume in the chair. If she actually fell asleep, the fiery tingling or numbness in her legs would eventually wake her up as the blood flow to her extremities slowed down. She was counting on it.

With her eyes closed, Simone's mind drifted to the life that awaited her in Galveston. She had really busted her ass to attain everything she had gained over the past ten years. Her life today had been earned and it gave her a sense of having a personal mission to fulfill. She was a living example that anyone could overcome the most heartbreaking unfairness that life could dish out. And she owed it to the kids she would eventually assist as a social worker to share her story and provide some hope to them. Pain and disappointment could be defeated in favor of a promising future, but sacrifices had to be made, goals identified, self-esteem firmly established. It could be done.

But the first person Simone had to help was her sister. Both of them had endured different forms of hell and Simone was convinced that Mona was in the midst of an identity crisis. Too proper, too stiff, too formal, too something that she hadn't quite put her finger on. Mona had forgotten who she was when they were growing up, the toughness that their neighborhood instilled, the independence that had marked her steps and perceptions when they were kids and teenagers. Simone hardly knew this person who slept in the other room with Sophie, the siddity woman who seemed more likely to crumble in the face of adversity rather than take a stand. And why? Because she had allowed money to become an integral part of her self-definition. On top of that, someone else's money, not her own. It was a complete 180 degree turn from what they had been taught as children and Simone felt responsible for reminding Mona of her roots before she corrupted her daughter with such destructive priorities.

Simone began to nod off as images of her childhood with Mona played in her mind. Because they were latchkey kids, Beatrice had been worried about their safety so their instructions were to go straight home after school and to lock the doors behind them. There were several more strict rules, the first one being that no boys were allowed inside the house if Beatrice wasn't at home. To ensure that they were too busy to get into trouble, the sisters were assigned daily house chores to complete along with their homework under the threat that Beatrice checked everything thoroughly, tolerating no form of filth anywhere in the house and no grades lower than B's on report cards. The house rules, while rigid, had reinforced self-discipline, without which Simone and Mona may have wound up as teenage mothers with multiple babies, high school dropouts, drug addicts, or something even worse. In an environment that promoted despair, disrespect, and violence, their salvation had been Beatrice's cumbersome rules. As an adult, Simone could appreciate Beatrice for showing no leniency about so many expectations, but she would never forgive the woman for letting her down when she needed her most.

A soft click disturbed the silence, but Simone thought little of it as she shifted in her chair. Then a pale light flickered across her face, sending an urgent message to her brain to open her eyes without moving any other part of her body. She remained absolutely still, watching as the door soundlessly swung open wide enough for a single, hooded person dressed entirely in black to slip through and close the door, restoring the room to nearly complete darkness. Simone's eyes had adjusted to the dim light hours ago so she had no problem keeping the intruder, who had failed to spot her, clearly in her sights. She continued to watch him, willing her heart and nervous system to remain calm as he slowly strode in the direction of Mona's and Sophie's bedroom. Beneath the blanket, her hand clutched the gun and she readied herself to fire. The moment that he had crossed the room and had his back to Simone, she released the gun's safety, eliciting a barely audible click, and raised the barrel to a level that placed his head in the crosshairs. The man immediately froze in his tracks, apparently having heard the faint threatening sound from behind him.

"That's right, asshole. Stay right there." Simone's voice was forcibly controlled as she cautiously raised herself to her feet, pushing the blanket onto the chair. She kept her eyes on the man's back and the gun leveled. "Now lean down slowly, put your gun on the floor, and step away from it." She was speaking too low to arouse Mona and Sophie. It would be a disaster if either of them was awakened and opened their bedroom door at this moment.

The nameless man appeared to comply with Simone's instructions, bending at his knees slowly with the gun nearly touching the floor. Then without warning, he dropped to one knee, swung around, and aimed the gun in the direction of Simone's voice so quickly that she barely had time to react before he fired. The silencer on his gun barrel effectively rendered his shots nearly mute, but when a bullet shattered the window behind Simone's head, the silencer became a moot precaution. Simone threw her body sideways, landing behind a sofa even as more bullets rained in her trail. She then scrambled on her hands and knees to find safety behind another armchair without him seeing her. She heard Mona call out from her bedroom and realized that she had seconds left to take out this lowlife before Mona came out of her room. Simone peaked around the back of her protective chair expecting to see the intruder coming toward her to finish her. To her shock, he was instead rushing to Mona's bedroom, resuming his mission before anyone else got in the way. His fingers were reaching for the doorknob. Reacting with a burst of adrenaline, Simone leapt to her feet, aimed, and fired three rapid shots into the man's head before he knew what had hit him. An instant later, the bedroom door was yanked open and the man's dead body, which had pitched forward against the door, fell onto the bedroom floor, almost striking Mona, who screamed as she jumped backward in her nightgown. All the lights in her bedroom were turned on and she had a clear view of the dead body sprawled headlong in her pathway before she saw Simone slumped in the armchair with relief and shock.

Mona's fisted hand flew to her mouth before she yelled to Sophie, who was also approaching the doorway, to come to her immediately. Mona then snatched up her daughter, hit the lights in the main area, and ran around the dead man to kneel in front of a limp Simone.

"Simone, what happened? Are you okay?" Mona held on tightly to Sophie, who had begun to cry upon seeing the lifeless man, as she spotted the shiny black gun in Simone's hands. "Jesus."

"I-I'm okay. He was goin' to kill you, maybe Sophie, too. I had to stop him."

There was a banging at their hotel room door and they both looked up with the same fear in their eyes. Then Simone's face became slack, her energy fully expended.

"It's probably Frank," she said in a dull voice. "You'd better call Harold before you let him in."

—⁂—

Harold and Nate stood near the dead body as the police crime scene unit videotaped the room and began to search for clues into both the man's identity and any connections he had to personnel at the hotel. Seemingly oblivious to all of the activity around him, Harold squatted down and slowly pulled the mask from the man's face.

"Mrs. Baker, would you mind stepping over here and seeing if you recognize this man?" Harold stood back up and pulled out a notepad.

Dressed in a black t-shirt and a pair of Simone's very casual, wrinkled linen pants, Mona slowly transferred Sophie into Simone's arms. Mona had been incapable of walking past the dead body lying in the pathway to her bedroom so Simone, who was around three inches taller, had supplied clothing that fit well enough under the circumstances. Both women were deeply concerned about Sophie, who had taken to sucking her thumb with her eyes tightly closed as she was shifted onto Simone's lap. More than anything, Mona was eager to be done with the police so she could whisk her daughter to certain safety far from the scene.

She crossed her arms and traipsed over to Harold and Nate, careful to step around kneeling CSU members and blood spatter on the carpet. Mona really didn't want to be anywhere close to the man who had attempted to kill her and Simone, but she knew that it was necessary. If she could identify him, she might also be able to provide a link to whoever wanted her dead. While everyone in the room assumed that Aaron was somehow tied to the murder attempt, without proof their unanimous assumption was worthless.

As Harold and Nate watched, Mona looked down at the man's face and frowned. Since he was lying on his stomach, the most she could see was his profile, but it was enough. "I've never seen him before."

"Are you sure?" Harold didn't seem surprised.

"Yes, I'm sure."

"Other than your husband, is there anyone else who you have reason to believe would want to harm you?" Nate's hands were on his hips. He looked disheveled, having obviously rolled out of bed in a rush to get to the crime scene as quickly as possible.

"No." Mona saw Nate and Harold exchange looks without comment. "But you two seem to have some ideas."

"It's not anything we're certain of at this point." Harold folded his notepad and placed it into a pocket on his shirt. "We suspect that your husband's associates may be behind this, though."

"Why?"

Again Nate and Harold swapped looks before Nate responded. "Because we've been monitoring all your husband's movements very closely since he was released and we don't believe he could have ordered this hit. I can't tell you more than that."

"So you think this was a professional hitman?" Like most people, Mona had seen it on TV shows hundreds of times, but never thought she'd ever be confronted with the possibility of being the target of a paid assassin.

"Don't think so. This guy was obviously a sharp-shooter, but still an amateur. Otherwise your sister would be dead. I got the impression from Simone that he was in a hurry. My guess is that he was in a hurry because he needed fast money." Nate leaned down and rolled up a shirtsleeve on the man's left arm. "He's got track marks."

"What does that mean?" Mona was mystified.

"He's a junkie with a habit to support. People like him will do almost anything to get money for dope. And it makes him more anonymous. Almost anyone could have hired him. We'll run his prints and try to locate his dealer. Whoever hired him could have found him that way." Harold grew yet more sober. "There's something else that I think you should know. Someone working at this hotel gave him a janitorial keycard to enter your room."

"Have you questioned Officer Costello about that? I mean, don't you think it's more than a little suspicious that he conveniently disappeared when this man got in?" Anger began to take hold in conjunction with heightened fear as Mona again acknowledged the reality that she could not trust the police to help protect her and her family. And thanks to this attempt on her life, there was no more room for doubt that Aaron was definitely guilty of something criminal.

"Frank was in the men's room when the prowler entered. He says that he couldn't have been gone more than three minutes."

"And you believe that?" Outrage now overtook Mona's fear. "Even after I've already warned you about Aaron's contacts around the city?"

"Hey, last time I checked, it wasn't illegal for a man to pee, lady," Nate interjected, obviously protecting his fellow officer.

"We'll be investigating Frank's explanation," Harold jumped back in while giving Nate a look that said cool it, "but we have no reason to doubt him at this time."

"Idiots. You're all idiots." Mona huffed disgustedly, hastily assimilating all the information as she grappled for a way to handle her first concern: Sophie.

"You're understandably upset, Mrs. Baker." Harold's voice was placating as Mona brusquely turned away to walk back to Simone and Sophie.

"We're leaving now, Detective. If you have any more questions, you can reach me on my cell."

"You and your family need to come with us. I've already made arrangements for you to be placed at a safe house where you can be guarded around the clock."

Mona angrily whipped back around to face Harold. "I thought that we were being guarded around the clock when I agreed to your protection two days ago. But it's like I said before, you can't help me. Aaron's corrupt friends are in some of the highest places and one honest cop can't protect my family from them."

"We can protect you a lot better if you're in a secure location. You've been tying our hands!"

"You just don't get it, Harold. And I'm tired of talking about it." Mona whirled back around to get Simone and Sophie, who were sitting on the bullet-ridden sofa located furthest from the corpse. "Let's go."

"Mrs. Baker," Harold called out, "you are still required to let us know where you can be reached."

"I'll let you know when I know." She cradled Sophie in her arms as Simone grabbed the duffle bag and suitcase she had packed after being interrogated by the police. They briskly walked past Nate and Harold without looking at either of them. When they reached the elevators, Simone pressed the call button and faced Mona.

"Where are we goin'?" It was around four o'clock in the morning, still pitch black outside, and the options were extremely limited.

Mona resignedly pulled out her cell phone and used the speed dial to make a call. "Jocelyn, it's Mona. I need a big favor."

—⁕—

The drive to Jocelyn's house was uneventful as Simone and Mona drove their separate cars, both women overwhelmed with physical and mental exhaustion. Sophie was fast asleep with her thumb still lodged in her mouth in the back seat of Mona's Mercedes, a status that Mona anxiously verified at each red light throughout the drive. Fortunately, Jocelyn, who had been a little too eager to have Mona's company despite the risky circumstances, lived in Meyerland, a well-to-do subdivision located around five or six miles from Aaron's home in River Oaks. The women had met at a coffee shop one morning nearly one month ago after Mona had dropped off Sophie at school. As soon as Mona had laid eyes on Jocelyn, who worked as a chief financial officer at a small printing company, she had been instantly drawn to her. Jocelyn had emanated confidence and power, qualities that never failed to stimulate Mona's attraction. Adding to her appeal was her voluptuous bombshell figure, which could hardly be concealed in the conservative beige Christian Dior pantsuit she had been wearing. Jocelyn was a blonde beauty queen who brought images of Marilyn Monroe to Mona's mind and she had been eager to win over the most recent object of her curiosity. Toward that end, she had begun stopping at the coffee shop each morning for a week until she and Jocelyn finally made small talk in line about the fattening desserts on display. As Mona had expected, they eventually exchanged phone numbers and days later were hooking up at Jocelyn's house during her lunch hours. They had shared highly charged, raw sexual encounters, experiences that Mona had found immensely pleasurable until Jocelyn had begun to show signs of an emotional attachment. Not wanting to end the affair just yet, Mona had hoped that maintaining distance from the woman for a while would help her to cool down. Now, only a week after implementing the distance strategy, the plan was going into the toilet.

Before arriving at Jocelyn's house, Mona had furtively called from her car to ensure Jocelyn understood the precarious situation inherent with both Sophie and Simone along. There could be no hanky panky, no feverish looks, no yearning touches. "Thank you for taking us in," Mona had said, "but this is purely platonic and only for a couple of days. I can't have my daughter exposed to the true nature of our relationship. Can you handle that?"

"Oh, yes, honey, anything you say." Jocelyn's breathless voice had prompted no confidence in Mona, but she could think of nowhere else to take her family on such short notice. She would have to make do for now.

Mona pulled up to Jocelyn's black security gate and soon saw the headlights of Simone's Jaguar behind her. A buzzer sounded and the gates slowly rolled back so the two women could drive up close to the front door, each veering their cars to the left and parking in a half-circle, fully lit driveway. Jocelyn was already standing outside in a red satin bathrobe to help with any items that needed to be carried into her five-bedroom home.

No sooner had Mona closed her car door before Jocelyn rushed over to steal a moment of husky whispers, radiating sex through her bathrobe. "Oh, baby, it's been too long. Look at you. I know you've been through hell, but I've missed you so much. Can I at least get a hug, a small kiss?"

Instantly put off, Mona stiffened and reached for her car door as though to open it. "I thought you understood that this is not that kind of visit." Her eyes flew to Simone, who was removing her baggage from her car at the moment.

"I know, baby, I know I said that, but now that I see you, all I want to do is touch you, kiss you, hold you." Jocelyn's eyes revealed a desperation that worried Mona as the woman pressed closer and closer, her lips only inches away from Mona's. "Just one little kiss. Please."

"This was obviously a mistake. I'm sorry to have bothered you with our problems." She again looked toward Simone, who was now holding her duffle bag and suitcase, standing a few feet away with a bemused expression on her face. "Simone, Jocelyn won't be able to accommodate us after all –"

"Of course I can! Don't be silly!" Apparently embarrassed, Jocelyn quickly stepped away from Mona and nervously ran her hands over her hair, which looked to have been freshly brushed before her company had arrived. "I just uh...I was saying hello. It's been a while since I saw Mona, that's all." She looked in the backseat and saw Sophie still sleeping soundly. "Do you want me to take Sophie in? I've prepared a room for her."

Mona hesitated for a few seconds, studying Jocelyn's body language closely. She was increasingly sorry that she had no real friends to call for help, just as Simone had stated the other day. The idea of being subjected to Jocelyn's disturbingly emotional behavior was the equivalent of volunteering for crucifixion in Mona's mind. Neither situation was agreeable to her in the slightest. Tonight, however, Sophie's comfort took precedence over Mona's so she was compelled to momentarily dismiss her reservations. "No, I'll get her."

"Okay then." The agony in Jocelyn's eyes betrayed her true feelings as she whirled around to face Simone, who hadn't budged an inch since noticing the strange interaction between Mona and the woman. "Simone, please pardon my manners. I'm Jocelyn Adams. Very pleased to meet you." She padded toward Simone with her hand outstretched.

At first, Simone seemed inclined to ignore the welcoming gesture being offered, but then she reluctantly shook Jocelyn's soft, milky hand. "I'm pleased to meet you as well."

"Can I help you with anything? Do you have any more bags?"

"No, this is it."

As the women talked, Mona retrieved Sophie from the car and began walking toward the front door of the house. Jocelyn uneasily looked at Simone and nodded. "I'll show you to your room then."

"Thanks."

—⁓—

All three women entered the house and closed the door securely behind them. The black gates secluding the property provided ostensible protection, but if the man who parked outside its borders had wanted to get inside, it would have been a cakewalk. For now, he was content to merely watch and remain invisible as he had been instructed. He was good at that. He was good at lots of things.

SIX

Although Jocelyn had prepped a bedroom for Mona, she had elected to instead share Sophie's room so she could keep an eye on her daughter. Sophie had clearly been traumatized at seeing the gory results of a fatal gunshot wound mere hours ago and Mona, who had witnessed a drug-related drive-by shooting in her childhood neighborhood, was ready to coach her child through the shock as best as she could. The world that Sophie had been nurtured in thus far was entirely different from the horrors that Mona had seen and become accustomed to living with each day until eight years ago. So Mona was prepared to get a child psychologist involved if necessary, sparing no expense to preserve Sophie's precious mental health.

At this time, Sophie was deeply asleep as Mona, still fully clothed, alertly lay beside her. Unlike her daughter, she had not been able to shut down her mind or her body. It was now approaching eight o'clock in the morning and Jocelyn had already left for work. Mona had been wide awake as the woman made the normal noises associated with taking a shower, later making coffee, donning heels that clack-clacked around the tiled hall-ways as she prepared to leave. When Jocelyn's car had finally been backed out of the garage and Mona heard the electric garage door rumble back down, a feeling of freedom from cruel punishment had briefly infused her being. It was the same way she had felt whenever Aaron left their house, which she and Sophie had more and more often occupied by themselves. She had felt re-lief, an irrational notion that now she could go out into the world and do...something. Of course, she had done absolutely nothing except screw around with willing partners of both sexes. She had nurtured no friendships, developed no academic interests, aspired to no career or volunteer activities. She had merely concentrated on raising Sophie, shopping, and finding new ways to please her libido, a carefree lifestyle that she had be-lieved she deserved after living in abject poverty for most of her life. She had paid her dues, been a model child and teenager, and for what? For fantasies of per-sonal accomplishment that Mama had preached, but never even achieved for herself. So why did she think that her daughters would do better? The same lack of opportunities that Mama had confronted was destined to be their stories as well. The world had not been at their feet! Drug dealers, child molesters, gangsters, and convicts had lived in the houses next door. In their neighborhood, most youngsters got out by either getting killed or going to prison.

As a teenager, Mona had been much different, tougher in many ways, ready to fight her way through the streets to get back home. Ready to protect Simone if anyone attempted to hurt her. She had not known any other mode of life or thought until Aaron came along and transplanted her to River Oaks, into safety and prosperity. Into comfort, plenty, and refinement. And after a long while, she began to relax, just a little at first, slowly letting down her guard. Because of her marriage to Aaron, Mona was able to observe a completely different culture and way of life, one that was actually accessible to her. And as more time passed, she had wanted to fit in, to belong, so she had purposefully changed, perfecting her speech, softening on the outside, losing the gritty drive that arose from constantly struggling to survive. Yet she had remained ever so distrustful of everyone, including herself. Some habits just couldn't be broken.

Mona rolled onto her back and stared at the ceiling. She had to think, to try to piece together all the information available to her about Aaron, the would-be murderer at the hotel, the people involved with trafficking the drugs. Mona was determined not to allow her thoughts to stagnate around the dead man's blood pooling around his head and drenching the carpet on the hotel floor not even five hours ago. This was not the time to ruminate on his gaping mouth and awful, lifeless eyes. No, she must focus on the critical questions that needed to be answered so she could survive. Where were the bank records that the police were so certain existed? Who was trying to kill her? Aaron or his drug partners? Or both? Only one thing was certain at this point. No one would be trying to kill her if the police were wrong about Aaron's drug activities. So she was likely to be in perpetual danger until his trial since the primary reason to kill her was to prevent her from testifying. And perhaps the sooner she died, the better because even the threat of her testimony could be temporarily paralyzing illegal business deals. Mona decided it was best – and extremely terrifying – to assume that everyone involved with Aaron's drug operations would want her dead.

She next forced herself to consider the timeline for Aaron's trial. If his attorney was any good, and her bets were that he was one of the finest in the field, then the trial date could be delayed for months, maybe even years. She was no legal expert, but she'd met plenty of attorneys who mingled with Aaron at business parties and heard them joke about filing so many briefs at courts that their cases were delayed indefinitely. They were proud of having been able to bottleneck the legal process for as long as possible if they believed the delays worked in their clients' best interests. Mona was not prepared to live her life on the run for a year or more, awaiting a trial that may or may not end in a conviction. She wouldn't put Sophie through that and she wouldn't gamble on her ability to keep them both alive that long. Something had to be done, but nothing crossed Mona's mind that she considered a viable solution. Her only options were unacceptable – run for an unknown amount of time or try again to trust the police. Either way, she was still obligated to find the bank records or Simone's life was over.

In the middle of her thoughts, Mona heard the doorbell ring and quietly got out of bed, careful not to awaken Sophie. She was expecting the clothes she had left at the hotel to be delivered. Since the exterior gates around the property were sealed, Mona dashed to a keypad near the front door and pressed a button that commanded the gates to open. She then immediately walked outside to meet the delivery person and help him carry in her belongings, vaguely noticing a white Ford Taurus parked across the street. The neighborhood was quiet as most homeowners were now sitting in their various cubicles and offices around the city. Despite last night's events, Mona fervently hoped that her family would be safe at Jocelyn's house, at least for the time being.

—⁓—

Upon stepping out of the shower, Mona could hear her cell phone ringing so she swiftly wrapped a large towel around herself and ran into the living room to grab the phone from her purse. Unfortunately, she still missed the call. She flipped the phone open, located the missed call function, and stared at the phone number. It looked familiar, but she couldn't immediately place it so she selected the call back option and placed the phone to her ear.

"Mona, I'm glad you called me back," a male voice stated.

"I'm sorry, who am I speaking with? I hit the call back button on my phone without knowing who would pick up."

"It's Richard. I heard about what happened last night and I wanted to check on all of you. How are you doing?"

"Oh, hi, Richard. We're fine, as well as can be expected, I guess. We're all a little rattled, but we'll get through it."

"Terrible thing that happened. Just terrible. I wanted you to know that my offer of help still stands. My wife and I could even give you a place to stay until things calm down."

"I haven't forgotten about your offer, Richard. I'm thinking about it."

"Great, my dear. You just let me know if you'd like to take me up on it. On another note, I understand from Detective Monroe that he's awaiting your new location information. What can I tell him?"

"Well, nothing really. I mean, we're staying at a friend's house in Meyerland right now, but we may be somewhere else tomorrow."

"Why don't you give me the address for where you are and I'll explain your situation to him. I'm sure he'll understand, but I must tell you that he's quite upset that you won't accept police protection. He asked if I could talk some sense into you."

"We've already tried his protection and look where that got us. Tell him you tried and failed. It's like having the fox ask for permission to guard the chickens."

"You can't believe that. Detective Monroe seems to be genuinely concerned about your safety."

"He probably is, Richard, but I don't think that his cop buddies feel the same way so we'll take our chances without them now. My mind is made up on it."

"Alright, Mona, alright." She could hear the resignation in his voice. "Have you had any luck locating the missing bank records?"

"No. If I had, you would have heard from me."

"Yes, I'm sure. Do you have any ideas about where to look for them?"

"I'm still planning to look at the house when I can. Something in my gut tells me that the records are there if they're anywhere at all. I've been slowed down, though, because Aaron hasn't returned to work yet. I don't want him to know that I'm searching the house."

"Yes, that would be best." There was a lull so Mona took the opportunity to give him Jocelyn's address. "Thank you, Mona. I'll pass this on to Detective Monroe and wait to hear from you. Be safe."

"Thanks, Richard. I'll be in touch." She ended the call and heard movements in the kitchen. Glass was clinking and water running. Simone had obviously been unable to sleep as well.

Mona went back into the bathroom, dried off, and then dug through her luggage, finding a pair of magenta cotton pants and an iron-free striped shirt to throw on. For the first time she could remember, she wished that she instead had blue jeans or anything more casual so she wouldn't feel so restricted. Her damp hair was wrapped in a shapeless ball on top of her head and held in place with a bright orange hairclip that matched nothing she was wearing.

Finally, Mona ambled into the kitchen where Simone was quietly sitting while sipping from a mug of freshly brewed coffee. She looked up when Mona entered. "There's some more coffee in the pot on the counter. Help yourself." She returned to her thoughts as Mona poured a cup and took a seat at the table with her sister. Together, they continued to sit in silence for a while.

"Are you okay?" Simone's spacey demeanor was unsettling Mona, whose frayed nerves were already approaching burnout.

Simone focused somber eyes on Mona's face as though seeing her for the first time that morning. "Not really. Are you?"

"No." Mona drank from her cup and then exhaled, resisting the urge to get a cigarette. "Last night was totally hellified and I have no idea what we're going to do."

"Yeah, I know." Simone began to stare into her cup. "Last night brought back a lot of memories, things that I don't like to think about."

"You mean Clarence?" Mona's remorse for her sister's past immediately haunted her soul again.

"Yeah. It's never easy to play God, bein' responsible for someone else's death."

"But you didn't have any choice last night."

"I had a choice ten years ago, though. Don't get me wrong, I'll never be sorry for killin' Clarence. But I can still see his face, the way his mouth dropped open before I shot him. Then he just sort of fell back clutchin' his chest and landed in his recliner. I thought he was dead when I went for his wallet, but he grabbed my wrist while my hand was in his pocket. I was scared shitless. But then he died. Just like that, it was over."

Mona could easily picture the scene that Simone described in her mind. Her thoughts inadvertently returned to the drive-by shooting she had seen at age thirteen and then the murderer at the hotel, but she commanded herself to black it all out. "I hate that you went through any of that."

"And I hate to tell you that the killin' probably ain't finished."

"What do you mean?"

"I mean Aaron." Mona squinted her eyes and shook her head with confusion. "He might need to be killed." Simone suddenly looked deadly.

"By who? Not you! And not me if that's what you're getting at."

"I'm not gettin' at anything yet, but you should start thinkin' about it. Somebody wants you dead and you may not survive unless we get to that person first."

"Oh no. No way."

"I didn't make up the rules, Mona, but I do know how they work and no prisoners are taken. Have you forgotten how the dealers shot at people on our block? And I met even more of 'em when I was hookin' and strippin'. It was bad enough seein' junkies sell their own children to get a fix, and the dealers...I saw firsthand how they would kill anyone, do you hear me? Anyone that they thought was a snitch or owed them money. Girl, you've got to face the reality that you're in their way right now. And that means that they probably want you in a coffin. Or maybe in the concrete of some new buildin' foundation."

Mona didn't respond. She couldn't even contemplate the line of action that Simone was suggesting. As before, silence fell between them. Then Mona was aroused from her thoughts by the crumpling sound of paper.

"Wanna tell me about this?" Simone slid the paper toward Mona, who immediately rolled her eyes upon reading the few written lines. It was a note from Jocelyn letting Mona know that there was plenty of food in the refrigerator and that she hoped they could discuss their relationship later that night.

"There's not much to tell. She's a fling." Mona folded the paper into a small square as she spoke.

"A fling. Okay, I get it. So are you a lesbian, or experimenting, or what?"

Mona remained mute, still toying with the paper in her hands.

"If you're embarrassed, don't be because, believe me, I've seen it all. Whatever is going on, I'm not judgin' you."

"I know that. It's just hard to talk about. My life isn't perfect."

"I think I've known that for a couple of days now."

Mona's mouth was a straight line across her face. "Yeah, I guess you have." She drank some lukewarm coffee as a stalling tactic. "I really don't know what I'm doing. All I know is that I've been living this way for so long, just going through the motions and keeping everyone at arm's length. Whoever comes along, ya know? Whoever seems to be in charge, to have control over their lives. Man or woman, it turns me on."

"So why do you think you're like that?"

"Never thought about it. It just is what it is."

"I don't think it's that simple. Wanna know what I think?"

"No, but I think you're going to tell me anyway."

"I think that you're attracted to powerful people because you want to be like them. I also think that you haven't liked yourself for a really long time. You're ashamed of what you are and where you come from."

"That's not true!"

"Oh yeah? Then why have you changed so much since we were teenagers? Why do you wear business suits instead of sweatpants to drop your kid off at school? And what's wrong with Sophie bussin' it like we did, come to think of it? You don't even talk the same. You sound like the rich white folks around here who probably don't have a single black friend they'd invite over for dinner. And yet here you are tryin' to be like them. Dressin' up to go get coffee, wearin' makeup to check the mailbox, doin' everything you can to help everyone overlook the fact that you're black and you weren't raised with no silver spoon in your mouth."

"You're wrong!" Mona hissed. "Maybe I have wanted to fit in, but that doesn't make me a sellout. I can't help it that I got lucky and married someone with money!"

"And I'm amazed that you would call it luck after everything that's happened!" Simone leaned across the table toward Mona. "Do you even have a black acquaintance, Mona? Tell me, because I really wanna know. Have you ever cheated on Aaron with a black person, male or female?"

Mona's eyes were flaring, but she didn't respond. The truth was that she couldn't remember the last time that she had been attracted to anyone who was black. Nor could she recall seeking out a black person's company for any reason in recent years. After living around so much threat throughout her formative years, she had been utterly relieved to escape it all with Aaron. The idea that she may have mentally condemned her entire race on even a subliminal level in the process had never occurred to her. Her first inclination was to dismiss Simone's accusation, but she hesitated because she had no evidence or argument to contradict the assertion.

"It's as if you've forgotten all the good people who watched our backs when we were kids," Simone continued. "The people who helped us live a little better. Do you remember when Mrs. Grady would drop off gumbo, greens, and peach cobblers because she knew Beatrice was workin' too much to make us a homemade dinner? Or Mr. Conners, the way he walked past the house every hour like he was guardin' us?" A combination of tenderness and anger suffused her voice.

"Yes, I remember. They were good to us," Mona whispered.

"Yeah, and they weren't the only ones. We have a lot to be proud of and grateful for despite some of the shit that happened to us and around us when we were kids. Look, we grew up in a rough neighborhood, there's no denyin' that. But the hard times we went through should have made you stronger, not all squeamish and two-faced. And certainly not ashamed to be the person you were until you married Aaron. You used to be this gigantic mountain of power, the kind that money can't buy. You were somebody to be reckoned with and I admired that! But now I feel like I hardly know you."

Mona frowned as she reflected on a childhood that she had come to regard as having been too hard, bitter, and violent. And while those perceptions were undoubtedly true, at some point in her life, the danger she had lived with had encompassed all of her memories. The loving people that Simone now spoke of had been erased, people who had definitely been goodhearted and deserving of much more reverence and warmth than Mona's memory had supplied. Why had she forgotten them? At a loss, she tilted her head backward and placed a palm at the nape of her neck to relieve the pressure that was building. She then quietly stared into the darkness of her mind with her eyes closed. "It's too much at one time. I just can't deal with all of this right now."

"I understand. I didn't expect you to. But you'd better get yourself together because we're up against some of the same types of sorry thugs that we knew in the hood. They're just not black and they sure as hell ain't poor."

Mona's cell phone began to ring, spoiling her ability to continue stretching her neck. Perturbed, she glanced at the caller ID screen, saw that the caller was Harold, and flipped the top open to answer the call. "Yes?"

"Thought you'd like to know that your husband is at work today."

"I'm on my way." She solemnly snapped the phone closed to end the call and stood up. "I need to leave. Aaron is gone to work so I've gotta get to the house as soon as possible. Would you please take care of Sophie for a little while?"

"Okay."

"Do you mind if I take your car?"

"No, go ahead. And be careful."

Mona sprinted down the hallway to put on a pair of shoes.

—◊—

After Mona had backed out of the driveway and watched the gates close, she took a few moments to survey the street around her. As before, it was quiet and, except for the unoccupied white Ford across the street, entirely empty. It was a reassuring sign, but Mona still dreaded being separated from Sophie and Simone. She felt suffocated with fear that something might happen to them before she returned and the mere thought nearly caused her to abandon the trip to Aaron's house in favor of remaining with her family. Before she could lose her nerve, she shifted the car into drive and headed toward River Oaks.

As she made the short five-mile drive, Mona continued to pay close attention to everyone and everything in the area, looking for anything that appeared out of the ordinary. Halfway to Aaron's house, she gazed in her rearview mirror and thought she spotted the same white Ford that had been parked outside Jocelyn's house all morning. Upon stopping at a red light, she stared in the rearview mirror again and then looked in the side view mirrors. Unfortunately, she couldn't see the driver because there were two cars separating them. The light turned green again and Mona slowly drove forward through the intersection, crossing over into the River Oaks subdivision. When she checked the rearview and side view mirrors again, the Ford was gone.

She sighed with relief and then admonished herself for being paranoid. Then again, she had every reason to be paranoid after surviving a murder attempt several hours ago. Forget what Simone had said about not being squeamish!

Mona rounded the corner to Aaron's house and parked one block away. Maybe this was more proof of paranoia since she was driving a car that Aaron wouldn't even recognize, but she didn't care. She walked briskly down the sidewalk toward the house carrying only her keys and her cell phone. To be prudent, she checked the garage for his car before entering the house through the back door. It was strange to be walking through the kitchen and living room areas as a trespasser.

Mona went upstairs to a room that had been converted into a library. Books were still strewn across the floor from the police's hardnosed search a few days ago. They had spared nothing and probably had no idea how valuable some of the books were that had been tossed so mercilessly to the floor. Mona stood in the center of the room and turned her head in a circle. She then stepped around the books and touched the bookshelves lining the walls, testing them for solid structures. Nothing budged. Disappointed but not surprised, she stared at the hardwood floors and wondered if there were any loose boards, a question she was not eager to spend time trying to answer since there had to be at least three-hundred boards in this room alone. Inspecting the floors for hidden compartments would definitely be a last resort.

Mona was heading to Aaron's bedroom when her cell phone rang. A glimpse at the caller ID screen revealed Harold as the caller again. She picked up the call. "What now?"

"Just wanted to know if you're there yet and how you're holding up."

"I'm here and I'm fine." She entered Aaron's room, which was obsessively neat, and decided to start with his closet. "Did you find anything about the druggie who tried to kill me last night?"

"Well, we questioned his mother this morning, think we got the name of his dealer, but we haven't located him yet. We're still looking, but there's a chance that he skipped."

"Great. More good news. Just what I need." She started opening the various drawers built into the closet wall. Socks, shoe polish, buffers. "So you're at a standstill then."

"Maybe, maybe not. We've still got some other leads to follow up on."

"Right." Nothing out of place in the closet. Mona walked back into the bedroom and stared at the floors. There had to be at least a thousand boards in here.

"Your attorney says that you're staying with a Miss Jocelyn Adams now."

"Uh huh."

"I gotta tell you, I just don't get it."

"Get what?" She went to the window and stared outside. He had a great view of the patio. The pool shimmered in the sunlight.

"What does a woman do for you that a man can't?"

Mona disgustedly snapped the phone shut to end the call, but Harold called right back.

"Sorry if my question offended you, but I'm still trying to understand. See, we've been watching you and Miss Adams since your relationship started and all us guys agree that we'd be honored to have a shot at either of you. But some women either don't like or want what men have to offer. Why is that? I'm just curious, if you don't mind."

Mona was more annoyed than offended. "What is this? Probe Mona's sexuality day?"

"Say what?"

"Never mind," she huffed. "Detective, my personal life is not under investigation and frankly I have no desire to enlighten you about the reasons for women's sexual preferences." Mona started examining the contents of Aaron's dresser drawers even though she knew the effort was futile. "What I'd like to know is how you happen to have time to call me with questions that are none of your business! Shouldn't you be chasing down those other leads you mentioned?"

"Nate is handling that while I watch your husband's building."

"Ah. Shoulda known."

"At the risk of offending you again, I want to tell you that you're a very attractive woman. You smoke too much, but you're very easy on the eyeball."

Mona stood upright and placed her hand on her hip. "Detective, are you hitting on me?"

"What do you think?"

"I think you don't stand a chance."

"Not if money is all that matters. We all know that you only go for people with money, which is weird since you only dump 'em anyway."

She snapped the phone closed again to end the call. She was walking into her former bedroom when the phone rang again. This time it was Simone.

"How's it going?" Simone immediately inquired.

"I've got nothing so far, but I'm still looking. Is Sophie up yet?"

"She's in the kitchen eatin' ice cream. I bribed her so she'd take her thumb out of her mouth."

"Good. Is she talking?"

"A little. I told her that the man on the floor had only been asleep because his head was hurt."

"Gosh, that was creative! Wish I'd thought of that."

"Yeah, well, it seems to have made her feel a little better."

"I'm sure she'll have more questions later. Would you tell her that I'll be back soon? And tell her I'm sorry for not being there when she woke up."

"I'll tell her. Talk to ya later."

"Okay." They ended the call as Mona stood in her closet. There was a pair of old jeans in here somewhere that she hadn't worn in years. She began sliding clothes around to find them. Her phone rang again and she checked the caller ID. Harold. "What now?"

"Bad news. Your husband left his office and appears to be on his way back to the house."

"Shit!" Mona increased the rate at which she rifled through the clothes, but then made the sensible decision to give up. She'd just have to buy another pair of jeans. "Where is he now?"

"Not too far from the house. It's only a three-mile drive so you'd better get out. He's hitting the gas like a pissed off NASCAR driver. His bosses must've told him to stay away for a while."

"But if that's the case, I can't leave yet. I may not have another chance to finish going through some of the rooms." Mona was panicking both because of Aaron's impending arrival and the idea that God only knew how long it would be before she could get in again to search the house.

"It's a waste of time anyway. Get out. He's almost there. If you leave through the back door, you'll be gone before he sees you."

Sudden resolve and stubbornness lifted Mona's shoulders. "No."

"No?"

"That's right, no. I'm staying. I'll just have to make sure he doesn't see me. It's a big house so it shouldn't be too hard."

"Christ, you're gonna give me a heart attack."

"Gotta go." Mona snapped the phone shut, turned off the light in her closet, and closed the door, hiding inside. She could hear her heart beating so loudly that it was like someone had put a microphone to her chest. Several minutes passed before she heard Aaron enter the house. She waited a few more minutes before cracking the door open a few inches. Mona could hear Aaron's voice, but she was too far away to make out what he was saying. He was on the phone downstairs in the living room. She took a few moments to muster some courage and stepped outside the closet, tippy-toeing across the hardwood floor in her sandals. Along with blue jeans, she really needed to buy some tennis shoes.

Once she reached the chest-high balcony that over-looked the living room area, Mona hunkered down to hear Aaron's conversation.

"I'm telling you that somebody is setting me up!" Short pause. "I don't know who, damn it, but there's no way I'd be stupid enough to keep blow in my house." Another pause. "You're right, you're right. We should meet, but I've still got a lot of heat all over me so it'll be a while." Pause. "There's nothing I can do about that right now. Haven't you been listening?" Pause. "I don't give a shit! My life is on the line here." Millisecond pause. "Listen, listen, hold on. Somebody's calling on my other line." Mona peeked over the wall just enough to see Aaron pacing in front of the patio doors as he talked. He was still wearing his business suit, but without the jacket. "Yeah? Tom! Well, you sure as hell took your time calling me back. I was escorted off my job around thirty minutes ago." More pacing. "Yeah, they just told me to leave." He paused and stared out the patio windows. "You told me that you'd take care of it so why am I jobless, huh?" Mona knew that tone of voice all too well. If Tom had been standing within range of Aaron's fist at that very moment, there would have been a personal introduction to Tom's face. "I'm coming to your office. You'll be there, right?" Pause. "Yeah, I'm leaving right now." Good! Mona would have more time to scour the house.

Just then, her cell phone went off with a muffled ring through her pants pocket due to an incoming call. She quickly ducked back down behind the wall just as Aaron's head whipped around at the noise. At the same time, she began striking, beating, and banging the phone against her leg to stop the ringing because her fingers were shaking too hard to hit the correct button.

"Give me thirty minutes." Based on the volume of his voice, Mona deduced that he was walking toward the stairwell, tracking the origin for the inexplicable sound.

Having finally stopped the phone's ringing, she scurried into her bedroom and frantically scanned the furnishings for something that would draw Aaron's attention. Something, anything that made noise. God, there must be something! Then she saw it. The music box! She ran to the dresser on which the antique wooden box rested, opened the lid, and heard the simple melody for "The Sun Will Come Out Tomorrow" begin to play.

"Fine. I'll see you shortly." He was upstairs in the hallway, maybe ten feet away from her bedroom when she slipped back into the closet and slowly closed the door behind her. Seconds later, Aaron was in the room and Mona held her breath. She couldn't see him, but she imagined that he must have walked over to her dresser by now and be staring at the box. He'd always hated that music box, which had been a wedding anniversary gift to her from his sister, Cheryl. Anything that symbolized their marriage drew his fury.

"Augh!" She abruptly heard objects hitting the floor, glass shattering, and then more items slamming against the walls. Throughout this violent episode, Aaron continued to grunt and yell meaningless noises, taking his frustrations out on everything he could get his hands on. She became worried that he might be compelled to fling open her closet door and start in on the items left inside so she pressed herself as far in the back as possible, burying herself behind old coats hanging in the most rear area. Although the closet consisted of around three-hundred square feet of space, Mona still felt exposed and the ongoing yelling beyond the door had made her bladder weaken.

Mona frantically flattened herself ever more closely against the closet wall. Every part of her being was trembling and she felt foolish for not leaving when she'd had the chance. Harold was probably parked outside watching the front door afraid for Mona's safety, but holding still unless there was a sign of something awry inside the house. She sure couldn't give him a sign from here! So she waited. And prayed.

Finally, after an eternal amount of time, Aaron suddenly became quiet. Mona was certain that the room had been destroyed and images of Aaron tossing her from the window upon discovering her presence played out in her mind. But then thankfully she heard him scamper from the room and rush back downstairs. Soon afterward, the back door was opened and shut so she knew he must have hurried out to make his appointment with his attorney.

Several more long moments passed before Mona found the nerve to crack open the closet door. Still frightened beyond all reason, she remained impossibly still until her cell phone rang from somewhere in the closet. She was momentarily jolted by the unexpected, blaring sound and raised her hand to her chest as though the gesture would calm down her heart. At the third ring, she quickly switched on the closet light and saw the phone lying at the back of the closet. When she finally answered the call, she was still wheezing lightly.

"Are you okay?" Yet again, it was Harold.

"I'm fine now that he's gone."

"And I'm right behind him."

"I know. He's going to see his lawyer." She was still struggling to catch her breath.

"Wish I could be a fly on the wall for that meeting. Hey, you don't sound okay."

"I am. I'm fine. I overheard him talking to someone on the phone before he left. He said that he's being set up by someone." Mona exited the closet and nervously looked around her former bedroom, which now looked as if a tornado had blasted through. She then walked over to her dresser and looked at the spot where the music box had once rested.

"That's what they all say." Harold sounded nonplussed.

"But has his suspicion been investigated? He sounded pretty believable, to be honest with you. As much as I loathe the man, I'd still hate to see him wrongfully convicted."

"It's not possible that he'll be wrongfully convicted. If we were wrong about him, you wouldn't be living in hotels or staying with Ms. Adams."

"Detective, if your department has had us under surveillance for a year, why did you decide to arrest him a few days ago? I mean, why not six months ago?"

He sighed. "Because we wanted an airtight case. We had plenty of evidence against your husband, but we still needed a physical link to him and the drugs. He's a smart man, Mrs. Baker, so tying him to the drugs hasn't been easy."

Mona thought about that. Aaron's intelligence was definitely above average and, like he said earlier on the phone, he was not likely to be stupid enough to store cocaine in his own house. "So back to my question. Why did your officers storm our house a few days ago?"

"We got lucky. Somebody called in an anonymous tip and told us that the coke was in there. We had a warrant within a matter of hours."

"Did you ever find out who called in the tip?" Mona was immediately doubtful of the source.

"No, of course not. I said it was anonymous, which was fine with us. We were just happy to finally get the bastard."

Mona wasn't so dismissive of this revelation, but begged the next logical question. "If you have such an airtight case, why do you need the bank records?"

"Because those documents will make sure we put your husband under the jailhouse. He keeps talking about somebody setting him up. Yeah, yeah, sure, sure. So if somebody is setting him up, why does he have a bazillion dollars in some offshore account that can't be linked to his job or any legal investments?"

"Yeah, I see what you mean." But the anonymous tip was still bugging her and the doubt was in her voice.

"Don't tell me that you're buying that crap about him being set up."

"Let's continue this later. I need to keep looking around while I can." Mona wasn't about to further drag out this conversation when she should be searching the house.

"Fine. But I don't like it." She could hear the frustration in his voice. "Call me if you find anything, which I still don't think will happen, by the way. The house is a dead end."

"It's only a dead end if you're wrong about Aaron." Mona ended the call and continued looking around the obliterated bedroom. The breaking glass she'd heard from the closet had been some crystal swan figurines that she had collected over a period of years. All of them were now smashed to smithereens. A few moments later she spotted a piece of the splintered music box lying in a corner on the other side of the room. Aaron had so much rage inside of him that it was eating him alive. And it was highly likely that this same rage was driving him to want Mona dead. The proof was in the state of her former bedroom since he had certainly been thinking of her when he had demolished it only minutes earlier. It was a horrifying reality to swallow.

By force, Mona's thoughts turned back to Aaron's phone conversations, during which he had stated that his life was on the line. Did he mean that his freedom was in jeopardy or that someone was trying to get him killed? She no longer questioned Aaron's guilt, but Mona was beginning to think that someone close to Aaron had wanted him put out of business. So now Mona had two additional questions to add to her growing list: Who wanted Aaron locked up or even dead and why?

SEVEN

A few hours later, a severely dispirited Mona was again sitting in Simone's Jaguar lighting a cigarette before starting the vehicle and leaving the River Oaks subdivision. She had had absolutely no luck, zero, zilch, zip, locating the godforsaken bank records that the police were hot on her to find. It just didn't seem fair. Surely God was up there somewhere looking down on her situation and rooting for her to get through it with continued breath in her body. She inhaled the nicotine. The fact that her breath might be polluted was a minor technicality. Breath was breath. Staying alive was staying alive. Sophie would not go through the rest of life as a motherless child.

Before giving up on her search of Aaron's house, Mona had used more than an hour to stare at the floors, testing select boards for secure placement and finding none that merited a closer inspection. As if she was an expert anyway! It had been a vain effort, all of it. And unfortunately, Mona was at a loss of where to look next. She would have to consider places in and around the house that may have escaped her and the cops' immediate attention. Once again, she resented being used by the cops against her will, but too much was at stake for her to look for a way out of it.

Depressed, Mona eased away from the curb and steered out of River Oaks. There was a Toys"R"Us store located near the house on Westheimer Road and Mona had decided to pick up the President Barbie doll that Sophie had been begging to receive at Christmas. Well, Christmas was definitely coming early this year. As far as Mona was concerned, Sophie could have Christmas every day if that's what it took to restore some semblance of her child's joy in the midst of their current transient lifestyle and the macabre scene she had witnessed last night.

As Mona drove toward the toy store, her eyes checked the rearview mirror several times to ensure that no suspicious traffic was trailing her. Nothing grabbed her attention, but she was not inclined to relax. She took a shaky drag on her cigarette as her mind drifted back to her narrow escape at Aaron's house when her cell phone had begun to ring at the most inopportune moment. For the first time, she wondered who had been calling so she clenched her cigarette in a death grip between her lips and grabbed her phone from the passenger seat where she had flung it after unlocking the car. According to the missed call function, the caller had been yet another jilted lover named Regina, who Mona hadn't seen since last year. Mona had no plans of ever returning the woman's call. In fact, Mona was more likely to cease all her frivolous bed-hopping in light of everything that was happening now. Somehow the life of casually stringing lovers along had lost its appeal and excitement, being upended by the stark reminders of late that it just wasn't real. Having a guy trying to put a bullet in your head while you slept – now that was real, as real as real could get.

She pulled into the Toys"R"Us parking lot and shut off the car engine. Even at two o'clock in the afternoon the parking lot was packed with the various expensive cars of wealthy suburban mothers with nothing better to do than shop while their husbands worked. She extinguished the cigarette, got out of the Jag, and walked into the bustling store with her focus being to get in and out with the Barbie doll in a matter of minutes. When she passed the checkout lines, however, she knew that the fast exit she wanted was not going to happen. She could expect at least ten minutes of just waiting in line to fork over cash for the doll. So that Simone wouldn't worry, she called to alert her sister to her whereabouts and promised to be back at the house within the hour. During the call, she learned that Sophie had again jammed her thumb in her mouth as she quietly watched cartoons. It seemed that her progress had gone in reverse.

Mona dwelled on her worries for Sophie as she walked the isles until locating the lengthy, well-stocked shelves full of every sort of Barbie doll that toymakers had been able to imagine: Beach Barbie, Executive Barbie, Formal Wear Barbie, and – there it was, finally – President Barbie. Mona chose the boxed doll closest to her reach and quickly headed to stand in the checkout line with the shortest queue. As she waited to pay for the doll, her eyes flickered over the people near her in case someone stood out as an outsider. Once again, she had no luck spotting anyone suspicious, but that didn't mean anything. She then noticed a few women conspicuously turning their noses up at her, causing Mona a brief moment of confusion before she remembered that her current clothing selection and hairstyle were hardly on par with the other patrons in the store. She looked down at her magenta pants and then touched the orange hairclip that still bound her long hair in a tacky, disheveled ball on top of her head. She must look homeless to the other people waiting to check out. A small smile creased her lips as she boldly met the stares of her critics, who quickly looked away with disapproving shakes of their heads. A few days ago, Mona would have been one of them so she had no illusions of what they were thinking. She was surprised to realize, however, that she could not have cared less.

After paying for the doll, Mona walked outside the store toward the Jaguar. The sunshine was startling compared to the bleakness that preoccupied her.

"Come this way or you'll be dead." A large, strong hand was suddenly clamped around Mona's left arm like a steel cuff and began pulling her in a direction away from the Jag. "And don't scream because then you'll make me very angry." The male voice was calm, heavy and disturbingly polite.

Ignoring the man's instructions, Mona began to yell for help while also swinging her purse at her captor's chest. "Let go of me! Help! Somebody, please! Let me go!"

The man roughly threw her to the ground and stood over her as she promptly rolled over to face him, lifting herself onto her hands while resting her butt on the scorching black asphalt. Petrified, she heaved frantically and locked eyes with him, certain that this was where she would die. The evening news would cast her as the recently estranged wife of a suspected dope-dealing Exxon-Mobil executive, probably the victim of a mugging that had gone terribly wrong. Her dying wish would have been for her daughter to have the damned Barbie doll resting untouched and still bagged beside her dead body in the parking lot when the police arrived. Witnesses would say that they had mistaken her for a homeless woman and were shocked to learn that someone of her financial standing had been dressed so poorly while shopping in their area. And poor Sophie would have been effectively deprived of the only parent she had been able to count on throughout her life. This final thought caused Mona to forget her fear as seeds of fury took root.

"What in the hell do you want with me!" She screamed at the man, who remained impassive as he continued to stare down at her. Mona got a good look at him, a fact that didn't seem to bother him. He was wearing dull colors that would easily make him forgettable or unnoticeable – a gray baseball cap, blue jeans, tennis shoes, and a gray t-shirt. His skin had the look of being permanently tanned and leathery as if he spent most of his time in the Sun. Precisely tapered brown stubble covered his cheeks and chin.

"You are one dumb lady. I'm trying to keep you alive, but maybe you deserve to die." He studied her face before purposefully surveying the movements of everyone around them. "I suggest that you call a cab rather than drive the Jaguar, Mrs. Baker. It's been rigged with a bomb." He tipped his cap and slowly walked away without another word, leaving Mona on the ground, still frightened but now confused as well as she watched him amble unchecked to the corner of the Toys"R"Us building and disappear without looking back.

Mona then took in everyone in every direction as she raised herself back to her feet. Despite her cries for help, not a single person had coming running to aid her in fighting off the unknown man. If his objective had been to kill her, she would've been a goner. Now that the imminent danger was passed, however, a sharply dressed, middle-aged woman approached her.

"Are you okay? I saw what happened and a few of us called the police already." The woman's eyes were sympathetic as she touched Mona's back.

"I'm fine, I'm fine." Mona's face showed no signs of gratitude. "Thanks." She reached down for her purse and pulled out her cell phone. As she flipped the top open to call Harold, she looked again at the lady, who was still patting her back with an expression of concern on her face. Mona's eyes traveled from the lady's face to the arm almost wrapped around her back, her incense increasing with each passing second. As she put the cell phone to her ear, she shrugged off the woman's touch. "You can leave now."

The woman gasped with surprise and shock at Mona's rudeness before stepping backward and strutting away with all the haughtiness that she could muster. As the woman left, Mona observed several other women onlookers also dispersing at once, probably deciding that Mona was one of the coarse ingrates that they despised most, one of "those people" who didn't appreciate their genuine passing kindness.

Mona continued to scrutinize everything and everyone around her as Harold's voice came on the line. "What's up?"

"You'd better get to the Toys'R'Us on Westheimer as fast as you can. A strange bird just told me that my car has a bomb on it."

"That's you at the Toys'R'Us? I just heard the call about a woman being attacked. A squad car is already on the way."

"Better send a bomb squad, too. I'd rather to be safe than sorry."

"Okay, and I'll be there as soon as I can. Nate will probably be there before me, but I'm on the way."

Mona ended the call and walked back to the Toys"R"Us entrance so she could watch for the police's arrival while being surrounded by as many people as possible, more for the appearance of safety than the prospect. She knew better than that now.

—⟋⟋⟍—

"According to the lead bomb technician, there's a bomb placed near the driver's side front tire. Would've taken seconds to attach to the car, but the perpetrator also would've had to stick around to set it off." Harold was standing with Mona, Nate, and several uniforms on the scene near the entrance to the Toys"R"Us store. Except for a few potential witnesses, all the customers had been evacuated, the parking lot cleared as much as possible, and the store temporarily closed pending the inspectors' findings. Now that a bomb had been confirmed, the store manager would be notified that the Toys"R"Us building needed to remain closed for the remainder of the day for everyone's safety as well as for the police's expediency. As of now, only the Jag and several police vehicles occupied the parking lot. It was hard to believe that Toys"R"Us had been crowded with customers just one hour ago.

Upon Harold's confirmation of the bomb, Mona felt her knees weaken and she inadvertently slumped forward against the detective. Without his arms to support her, she would have soon been on her knees as she contemplated the fact that someone had nearly succeeded in depriving her of raising her child, of truly celebrating her sister's return and acting on the life changes she was beginning to desire. It could all have ended an hour ago in a massive explosion that mutilated her entire body beyond recognition in a single instant. Mona buried her head in Harold's chest and began to sob as he held her under Nate's stoic glare.

"It's alright, Mrs. Baker. Everything will be alright."

Mona continued to cry without interruption, letting all the pent up emotions be released from her psyche and her soul. It had been building up in her since the police had burst into her home a few days ago and she couldn't hold it all in for another moment longer. Her life had been forever changed in a terrifying way that had shaken her free of her prized stability and the financial windfall that Aaron represented. She felt like an apple that had been plucked from its tree before having fully ripened. If the laws of karma were at work, then Mona could admit to herself that she probably did deserve some of the troubles that had befallen her. After all, she had hardly been a model woman, having married for money and later gone on to guiltlessly bear the illegitimate child of one of her lovers. And she couldn't even count the number of lovers she'd snuck around with throughout the entire duration of her marriage. The strange man had suggested that maybe she deserved to die because she was a dumb lady. At this moment, a part of Mona agreed with him: she was a dumb lady. But her love for Sophie prevented her from also agreeing that she might deserve to die for this reason. For Sophie, Mona resolved that her survival was not an option. Perhaps Simone was right – others would need to die so that Mona could go on living.

"So are you ready to move into the safe house, Mrs. Baker?" Nate's heartless tone of voice penetrated Mona's personal pity party. "The way I see it, we're the only option you've got."

Mona had no more tears inside of her. She lifted her head away from Harold's solid chest and stepped away from him while wiping her face with her hands. "No, I already told you. No safe houses."

Nate placed his hands on his hips and stared up at the sky for a moment, obviously trying to control his temper and impatience. "Maybe you just wanna die, is that what it is?"

"No, Detective. I can't move into a safe house because I want to live." She was beginning to feel a supernatural calm overtake her. Her mind began to clear, rationality began to set in, emotions began to dissipate. It was necessary in a war zone and had been a way of life in her childhood neighborhood. Her ability to resurrect this frame of mind had not entirely abandoned her, she now realized. It had simply grown flabby like an unused muscle. But the events of the past twenty-four hours had reactivated her need for the muscle and so she must learn how to use it again. Mrs. Baker did not need the muscle, but Mona did. "By the way, why don't you call me Mona. I'd prefer it." She looked at Harold, who also seemed put off by her continued refusal of police protection. "Would you please drive me back to Jocelyn's house? I need to check on my daughter."

"Sure, I'll take you, but I'm telling you right now that I've already stationed two uniforms at the house to protect you, your daughter, and Miss Edwards until we believe there's no longer a need."

"I've already told you –"

"I don't care what you've told us! My decision is final. You're not the only one who can be stubborn. Now let's go."

When Harold and Nate escorted Mona into Jocelyn's house, Simone clutched her sister in a bear-like hug. "Are you okay?"

"Yes, I'm fine."

"Are you sure?" Simone examined Mona's face.

"I'm sure."

"Alright. I guess I believe you." She squinted her eyes as she continued to look at Mona. "You look different."

"Miss Edwards, your car is still in the Toys'R'Us parking lot with our bomb squad and the CSU. We'll most likely keep the vehicle impounded for several days as well." Harold remained near the doorway with Nate as he spoke.

"That's fine. I don't care about the car. Keep it as long as you need to."

"Where's Sophie?" Mona was disappointed that the child hadn't already greeted her.

"She's sitting in front of the TV with a popsicle."

Mona immediately left the room to check on Sophie's condition.

"Miss Edwards, we've already informed your sister that two officers will be stationed outside this house for as long as you all are here. These officers have also been instructed to escort you everywhere should you leave the premises because we're extremely concerned about your safety. Try to stay together as much as possible and, if you must leave the house, confine your outings to public places with a lot of people around."

"Of course, we would still prefer that you all reside in a safe house since we would have more control over –"

"No thanks," Simone cut off Nate. "I think my sister has made that clear."

"But maybe she would listen to you if you told her –"

"Uh uh. Not gonna happen." Simone walked to the front door and opened it. "Thank you, gentlemen, for bringin' Mona back and assignin' two of your finest to our care. We'll call ya if we have any updates that you may find useful."

"You'd better hope your sister finds those bank records," Nate leaned in on Simone. "Cuz if she doesn't, I'll be coming for you myself. Count on it." He wheeled around and walked out the door without another word as Simone watched. She clutched the doorknob so tightly that her arteries popped up beneath the skin on her hand, but she showed no other visible reaction to Nate's threat. Simone was definitely afraid that Aaron's drug money might never be found, but she was more afraid that her sister might get killed regardless of the money.

Harold reached the threshold, but turned to face Simone once more before crossing over it. "You and your sister are making a huge mistake, Miss Edwards. I hope that you'll reconsider our offer before it's too late." His grave facial expression couldn't have been more transparent with worry. He held Simone's gaze for a fraction of a second longer before exiting the house.

Simone closed and locked the door. She then went to a window to watch the detectives leave as well as to get a look at the policemen currently stationed in a squad car outside the property gates. Jocelyn was not likely to react favorably to this new development and the danger that it inferred. Simone and Mona would need to make other living arrangements as quickly as possible.

Simone went into the living room where Mona was now sitting cross-legged on the floor with Sophie in her lap. The two seemed to be whispering to each other and Simone saw Sophie nodding several times, an encouraging sign. Rather than interrupt them, Simone decided to get dinner started. It would be a gesture that Jocelyn might appreciate, coming home to a hot meal after a long day at work. And it would exemplify her guests' gratitude for her hospitality on such short notice. She decided on lasagna, salad, and garlic bread. After dinner, Simone would wait until Jocelyn and Sophie were asleep before speaking at length with her sister about the car bomb, her mysterious guardian in the parking lot, and a risky idea she had come up with to keep her sister alive.

—⁂—

Jocelyn flew through the front door later that evening like a whirlwind that had spun out of control. "What's going on? Why is there a patrol car parked in front of the house?" She received no responses and so hurried into the living room, where she found no one. She then followed the scent of lasagna to her kitchen, where Simone was pulling the steamy dish out of the oven.

"Ah, Jocelyn. We've been waiting for ya so we could all have dinner together. Why don't you put down your purse and briefcase so you can help me with the salad and breadsticks?" She had heard Jocelyn in the entryway and chosen to ignore the woman until the aroma of food and Simone's extremely calm disposition could work together to counter her host's anticipated mania. Simone smiled warmly as she spoke, placing the lasagna on the stove before closing the oven. "The salad is in the refrigerator. I hope you like Caesar style."

"Y-yes, I do." Jocelyn mechanically went to the refrigerator to get the salad. "Why are the police parked outside my house?" Her voice was less panicky but still uptight.

"They're insisting that Mona needs round-the-clock protection so they can sleep better. It's no big deal." Neither Simone nor Mona would be discussing the car bomb incident with Jocelyn.

"Why are they suddenly insisting upon that?" The women were now walking into the dining room, Simone carrying the lasagna and Jocelyn carrying the salad as they continued talking.

"It's not sudden. They've always wanted it, but Mona refused. Now they're here despite her refusal. That's all." Simone lowered her voice as though sharing a secret. "To tell you the truth, I think that one of the detectives has a crush on her and he's just tryin' to make sure she doesn't get around, if you know what I mean."

"Well, that's just ridiculous." Jocelyn's instant jealousy immediately preempted her concerns just as Simone had hoped. "He can't have officers posted outside my house unless he thinks there's some sort of imminent danger." She contemptuously set down the salad on the table. "I think I'll go outside and ask the officers to leave."

"No! You can't do that!" Simone had already placed the lasagna at the center of the table. Her feigned distress was perfectly executed as she faced Jocelyn from the other side of the table.

Confused, Jocelyn halted all movement. "Why not?"

"Because," Simone now looked conspiratorial, "I think one of 'em is kinda cute and you'll be ruinin' things for me, that's why not." It was a complete lie. In actuality, Simone didn't want to risk the policemen saying anything about the car bomb to Jocelyn. Although the story had been covered on the evening news, the police had protected Mona's identity from the reporters. And luckily, Jocelyn had been too startled at seeing the police in front of her house to notice that Simone's car was missing.

Jocelyn's expression relaxed now that she thought she was in on a secret. "Oh, alright. I guess it doesn't hurt to have them around then." They walked back into the kitchen, at which point Simone placed the breadsticks in the oven while Jocelyn selected several salad dressings from the refrigerator. "So which one has caught your fancy?"

"The one sittin' on the driver side. I haven't gotten a close-up look yet, but I'm plannin' to take them some dinner later tonight."

"I'm sure they'll appreciate that." Jocelyn smiled as she walked back toward the dining room. "Where are Mona and Sophie?" She paused before exiting the kitchen.

"Mona's readin' her a book in the bedroom. Would you mind tellin' 'em that dinner is being served?"

"Sure. I'll tell them right now. Everything smells delicious, Simone." She smiled as she left the kitchen.

Simone also smiled. She had brilliantly diffused Jocelyn's predictable – and understandable – fears, which meant that Jocelyn wouldn't be putting them out tonight. And tomorrow, Jocelyn would have her house back to herself if Simone managed to talk Mona into her plan of action.

—⚊—

Dinner was uneventful, the conversation somewhat trite, mostly being limited to the subject of Jocelyn's CFO job – as if anyone at the table other than Jocelyn was actually interested in the topic. But since the last thing the sisters wanted to discuss was the increasingly lethal danger that Mona was in, they both managed to appear especially intrigued with the pitfalls and importance of Jocelyn's relentlessly boring occupation. Throughout the dinner, Sophie picked at her food, taking only a few bites here and there, but Simone blamed herself for the girl's poor appetite. Simone had been feeding her every sort of junk food in the house all day so the child would take her thumb out of her mouth and maybe talk. Thankfully, Sophie seemed to have made significant progress since Mona returned from Toys"R"Us, but she still wasn't back to her normal sprite self. The Barbie doll seemed to have worked some small amount of magic, though, and it was now situated on Sophie's lap as she used her fork to move her food around her plate.

After an acceptable amount of time had passed, Simone excused herself and Sophie, taking the girl into the bathroom for her evening bath. It wasn't long after they had left the room before Jocelyn broached her concerns with Mona. The two women were sitting on opposite sides of the table facing each other directly.

Jocelyn peered into Mona's eyes. "Simone tells me that one of the detectives investigating your husband has a crush on you."

"Oh, yeah. That's nothing. You know how it goes." Mona rolled her eyes in a dismissive manner.

"Yeah. I guess I do know how it goes because I've got a crush on you, too. But you don't seem to want me either." The normal moistness in Jocelyn's eyes suddenly increased precipitously, threatening to transform into tears, but to Mona's relief none fell.

Mona nodded her head at Jocelyn's pained accusation. She had already made up her mind to be honest with Jocelyn about her feelings. In truth, she had never lied to Jocelyn, but she also had never forcefully corrected any erroneous assumptions the woman had made during their relationship. It had been easier to keep the fantasy alive that way, allowing Jocelyn, as with the many other lovers Mona had known, to think whatever she wanted to think. But Mona had certainly at no point communicated some long-lasting intention of being with Jocelyn or anyone else outside of her marriage.

"You're right, Jocelyn. I don't want a serious relationship with you. That's the truth. It's also the truth that I don't want a serious relationship with anyone, not even the man I've been married to for eight years.

So don't take it personally. Believe me, it's not you. It's me. It's the way I grew up, it's how I lived as a teenager, things I saw people do to each other. I honestly don't think that I have the mental or emotional capacity to love someone and want to be with that person exclusively for the rest of my life."

"Then why did you start things up with me? Was I just something to do? A plaything to relieve your boredom?" Jocelyn had quickly shifted into a contentious, defensive mode.

"I'm sorry, Jocelyn, but I thought you understood that I was married and not looking to get divorced at the time. I thought we could have a little fun together, ya know? I thought you might be a little bored just like I was. It was never supposed to get serious. And I certainly wasn't looking to hurt you." Mona broke eye contact with Jocelyn, unable to withstand the sustained anguish in the woman's eyes. "Look, I'm sorry if I misled you. I've always tried to be as upfront as possible, but it's obvious that I failed you that way."

Tears finally escaped Jocelyn's eyes as she continued to look at Mona miserably. She nevertheless regained her composure well enough to speak in a very controlled voice. "Mona, your family is lovely and it has been a pleasure to share my home with you, but I want you all out tomorrow before I get home from work. Is that understood?"

Mona nodded without looking up. "Yes, I understand. Thank you for opening up your home to us, Jocelyn. You've been very kind." Mona knew that Jocelyn considered her to be a miscreant at that very moment and she counted her blessings that she didn't ask them to leave tonight. If she had known the truth, that a bomb had been planted on Simone's car that afternoon, she probably would have ordered them to pack and leave right now rather than waiting until tomorrow.

Jocelyn remained silent and exceedingly still for a few seconds before pushing her chair back from the table and leaving the room. With her host gone, Mona sighed, stood up and began to clear the table of all the dishes. The kitchen was already spotlessly clean thanks to Simone. Mona only needed to load their used dinnerware into the dishwasher, a task that she dutifully executed.

In light of both the attempted car bombing and Sophie's mental condition, Mona had planned to ask that Jocelyn allow them to stay one more day so she and Simone could make a well-thought-out plan rather than continuing to leap from residence to residence. But yet another turn of events had wrestled away any of her ideas about controlling her circumstances. Remarkably, though, Mona was fine with it. She was beginning to trust in a much different, former version of herself that was surfacing for oxygen after having been buried so many years ago.

EIGHT

Much later that evening, Mona was lying in bed with Sophie and waiting until the child was sound asleep before leaving the room to speak with Simone. Not long after Sophie began to breathe deeply, there came a soft knock at her door. Guessing that it was Simone, Mona slowly rolled off the bed and crept outside the room, slinking with Simone to the guest bedroom that her sister had been assigned. In a way, it was rather funny how far they had to tiptoe in silence before reaching Simone's bedroom, which was located on the opposite side of the house in quarters that could have been reserved for a maid who needed to remain out of sight. Without sharing their thoughts, both sisters had already assumed that Jocelyn had wanted Simone as far from Mona's room as possible so there would be an opportunity to couple with Mona without interruption. Now a bitter Jocelyn understood, however, that her rooming calculations had been pointless.

When the sisters finally reached Simone's bedroom, they huddled together on the bed. They then spoke softly even though there was no way that Jocelyn could overhear them from her bedroom, which was a single door away from the room in which Sophie slept.

"So tell me about this guy that grabbed you at Toys'R'Us."

Mona had been thinking about him almost nonstop since Sophie had fallen asleep. "Do you remember the man I told you about who was standing across the street near the jail?" Simone nodded. "Well, this guy was wearing a baseball cap just like that man. I can't help wondering if it was the same person. He saved my life, but he didn't tell me his name, why he did it, nothing. But he knew my name, called me Mrs. Baker. It was weird."

"Okay, so maybe he's an undercover cop that Harold has followin' you without you knowin'. I could see him doing somethin' like that since he and Nate keep pressin' us to accept police protection."

"He didn't mention anything like that when I told him about the man."

"As if he would tell you! He probably doesn't want you to know because they're still investigatin' you without your knowledge or somethin'."

Mona was skeptical of Simone's train of thought. "No, I don't think so. Harold has been looking out for me these past few days. I think I can trust him, but I'm not so sure about Nate. There's something about him that I just don't like."

"You mean, the fact that he's a royal asshole maybe?"

"No, no. There's something else about him that bugs me. Like he hates me, especially when I repeat my feelings about living in a safe house. He acts like it's a major inconvenience to him. And now I'm beginning to wonder if it's an inconvenience because he wants to hem me off somewhere to be killed more efficiently."

The sisters somberly chewed on this possibility in silence for a few minutes before Simone made a personal leap of logic. "So maybe Harold suspects Nate, too, which is why another undercover cop is followin' you around and helpin' you out."

"Maybe." Mona nodded her head and considered a deeper appreciation for Harold.

"And maybe Harold didn't tell you because he's actually trying to collect evidence that might incriminate his partner. He'd really have to keep that on the down low."

Once again, Mona nodded, but she wasn't ready to draw any conclusions about her unexpected guardian.

"What about the bomb? Do you think Aaron is behind it or his drug buddies?"

"There's no way of knowing yet. Harold says that they're going to review the parking lot surveillance cameras to try to identify the person. No guarantees, though." Mona's voice quivered as images of an explosive demise overtook her mind yet again. If it hadn't been for her mysterious sentinel, she wouldn't be sitting here now.

"Aaron is in bed with some really vicious jerks!"

"Yeah, his drug bosses are supposedly part of a Columbian family named the Escobars."

"Who told you that?"

"The police did when we discussed my testimony a few days ago."

Simone's eyes became distant. "Escobar, Escobar...I know I've heard of 'em before." She stared at the bronze-colored comforter on the bed. "I can't remember when or where I've heard of 'em, but it can't be good."

"What, did they kill somebody you know?" Mona's anxiety level was abruptly amplified to the millionth power.

"I don't remember. I hate when that happens."

Mona quietly watched her sister's face contort in various expressions of frustration as she struggled with her memory to no avail. "Well, maybe it'll come to you later."

"Yeah, we'll see." Simone sighed and shook her head. "Meanwhile, we need to get outta here."

"How'd you know?"

"Know what?"

"That Jocelyn wants us to leave tomorrow before she gets home from work."

"She does? When did that happen?"

"After dinner." Mona tilted her head to the side. "So you didn't know?"

"No, but that's okay because we were leavin' anyway. I've got a plan to run by you tonight."

―◊―

The following morning, both Simone and Mona were wide awake and wired up in their separate bedrooms as they listened attentively for Jocelyn's departure. The minute their host was gone, they sprang into action, making phone calls to various people, arranging the specific timelines for the plan they had agreed on last night, and loading Mona's Mercedes with their belongings. As they sat down for an early lunch, Mona's cell phone rang. She wasn't surprised to see that Harold was the caller since the police monitoring the house would have notified him of the Mercedes being packed.

"Are you and your sister planning to move today?" Harold didn't waste any time with pleasantries.

"As a matter of fact, yes. We're moving to the Intercontinental Hotel downtown this afternoon. Things are a little too cramped here, if you know what I mean."

"Oh really? So I take it that you and Miss Adams are on the outs now."

"Yep, we're on the outs." Simone looked at Mona and rolled her eyes. Harold was becoming typical.

"How are you feeling?"

"I'm alright."

There was a short pause. "You sound weird."

"Weird how?"

"I don't know." He paused again. "I get the feeling that something's going on that you're not telling me."

Mona sarcastically tisked into the phone. "You're wrong. Have you forgotten so soon that I was nearly blown up yesterday?"

"No."

"How is a woman who was nearly blown up supposed to sound, Detective?" Mona's voice had the ring of boredom. She began to watch Sophie eat the SpaghettiOs that Simone had heated up for her.

"That's a stupid question."

"Okay, then let's try another one. Who is the weirdo that you've got following me around town?"

"Now what are you talking about?" Harold was becoming annoyed.

"You know perfectly well what I'm talking about. The man I told you about at Toys'R'Us yesterday. The man who's been parking outside Jocelyn's house since we got here. I'm not blind." Mona was testing Harold's reaction to determine if he might actually be responsible for keeping her alive. She didn't truly know if the unidentified man had been watching Jocelyn's house, but it seemed to be a fair guess since he knew her name and had obviously followed her to the toy store.

"Your guess is as good as mine, Mona, as far as that guy goes. We don't have any leads on him yet."

"Is that so?"

"Yeah, that's so. Trust me, I wanna know who he is just as much as you do, but right now, we got nada."

Mona didn't know whether to believe him or not. His voice gave nothing away over the phone.

"Back to my original line of questioning. Why are you moving into another hotel? Do you actually think that's a good decision given what happened a couple of nights ago?" There was palpable incredulity in Harold's voice.

"There's nowhere else for us to go. We'll take the necessary precautions this time."

"And you can believe that we will as well."

"I figured as much."

"What time are you planning to check in?"

"This afternoon. First, we're going to stop off for lunch at La Cocina."

"You sure are taking a lot of unnecessary risks. I just don't get you at all."

"And you never will, Detective."

He sighed. "I didn't mean it like that, Mona."

"But I did."

"Fine. Anyway, my guys will be with you every step of the way today to make sure you're safe. Call me if you need my help with anything." Harold hung up without waiting for Mona's response.

Mona snapped her phone closed and wordlessly exchanged looks with Simone, who was eating some leftover lasagna. They had a very dicey day ahead of them and so far everything was going as planned.

———

At noon sharp, Simone, Sophie, and Mona were in the Mercedes and leaving Jocelyn's house for the last time. The sisters waved at the two cops parked near the security gate as they pulled out of the driveway and proceeded down a street that would take them out of Meyerland and toward the Galleria, a large, multilevel mall located around ten miles away. Situated in a popular area of town, not only was the Galleria consistently overflowing with heavy traffic and activity, but it contained a terrific selection of excellent, well-frequented restaurants, including La Cocina, where they were headed.

Mona glanced in the rearview mirror to confirm that the police officers were in tow in accordance with their instructions and then put on her sunshades. She and Simone rode in silence while Sophie listened to her favorite Mariah Carey CD in the back seat.

The uniforms assigned to Mona were following closely behind them every mile of the way to La Cocina. Since it was a workday lunch hour, Mona needed several minutes to locate a parking spot near the restaurant. The police, on the other hand, merely watched them park and then followed them in the patrol car to the restaurant entrance. One of the officers then got out of the car to follow the sisters into La Cocina while the other officer hastily parked in a place reserved for handicapped persons before also entering.

Inside La Cocina, there was a crush of bodies in a small waiting area. Unsurprisingly, since the Galleria was surrounded by a large, bustling business district, most of the patrons were dressed in business suits. Mona had already called ahead to make reservations so she, Simone, and Sophie were soon ushered to a booth near the back of the restaurant as the police officers continued to stand guard near the entrance. One of the men steadily scanned the restaurant while the other officer kept his eyes on Mona.

—ɯ—

As Mona reviewed a menu, her unnamed guardian surreptitiously entered the restaurant and took a seat at the bar where he could easily see her. As he had stated in the Toys"R"Us parking lot, this lady was undoubtedly a dumb one. Why in hell, he thought to himself, would she place herself in such prominent danger by coming to this place and making it particularly difficult for her police guards to protect her? Any number of options was open to her stalkers – another bomb, food poisoning, a fatal stabbing. Were his instructions of a different nature, he would be laughing in his beer with glee at his luck right now. Really, did they come any dumber than this one?

Now what was she doing? Looked like she was taking her daughter to the restroom. He watched her motion to the police officers and point toward the restroom as she ushered her daughter in that direction. One of the police officers nodded and proceeded to follow them, choosing to post himself a short distance from the door after Mona and Sophie went inside. The man looked back toward the table where Simone was still sitting. When a waiter approached to deliver drinks, the two began to talk, gabbing as if they had known each other for years. Then Simone stood up and hugged the young lady. Must be some long lost friend, he thought as he judiciously sipped his drink. As the waiter continued talking to Simone, she pointed toward the kitchen. Simone's facial expression changed to one of surprise as she nodded. She then set down her table napkin and began to follow the waiter to the kitchen as they continued talking and laughing like old pals. Mid-stride, Simone turned toward the cop watching her and waved to let him know that everything was fine. The poor guy was obviously torn between two evils: either follow Simone to ensure her safety or continue watching the door and monitoring the people within the restaurant for any potential dangers. In the end, he chose to stay where he was, probably since Mona, not Simone, was perceived as the one whose life was in peril. The cop pressed a button on the walkie-talkie attached to his shoulder to notify his partner of the development. He then crossed his arms and stood his post, his eyes roving the restaurant like Arnold Schwarzenegger's character, the Terminator, searching for his primary target, Sarah Conner. Meanwhile, Simone continued laughing with her waiter friend as she vanished into the restaurant kitchen.

A few minutes passed by as the man waited for Mona and her daughter to reappear from the restroom. He began to get a little antsy, glancing at his watch and then at the police officer still standing outside the restroom door. This was getting weird. How long did it take for a little girl to pee and wash her hands? Five minutes? Six maybe? He glanced at his watch again. It had been nearly ten minutes since Mona had taken Sophie into the restroom. He saw that the cop was also getting uneasy. The officer began talking to different women entering and exiting the restroom, looking more and more puzzled with each passing second. Soon afterward he poked his head into the restroom. What the hell? Something was up.

The man stood up and pressed his way through the crowd to the restrooms so he could hear what the police officer was saying to the women coming to and from the restroom. From what he could gather, the women were saying that no one fitting Mona's and Sophie's descriptions was inside. As the officer dashed into the restroom, the man turned around and exited the restaurant, trotting to the spot where Mona had parked her Mercedes a short time ago. The car was still there.

He then ran back into the restaurant and saw both police officers searching the area, going from table to table and peering at the occupants. With each passing second, they were increasingly hurried and frantic as they rushed about the restaurant. Finally they jogged through the waiting area toward the kitchen, the crowd parting as though the cops were Moses commanding the Red Sea. People couldn't move out of their way fast enough, barely avoiding being shoved aside as the cops ran with their hands straight out in front of themselves to get through. When they disappeared into the kitchen, the man exited the restaurant once again and went around to the back to observe their exit. Based on their body language, he would know whether the sisters had been located.

Shortly afterward, the cops burst from the kitchen back door, one of them yelling into his shoulder walkie-talkie that they had lost their subjects. Damn! He discreetly darted from car to car, quickly looking inside a few of them with the futile hope of seeing the women hiding. He instinctively knew, however, that the effort was ridiculous. Somehow, the sisters had figured out a way to outsmart their cop custodians, who they obviously considered a burden for some reason. In the process, they had also left him behind with no way to guess at where they had gone or what they might be doing. Maybe Mrs. Baker wasn't so dumb after all.

NINE

Now riding in a black Range Rover, Mona, Simone, and Sophie were speeding away from La Cocina only twenty minutes after entering the restaurant. Their plan to ditch the cops had worked like a charm.

"Boy, Lyle sure did come through!" Simone was sitting in the passenger seat wearing a brunette wig of braids and a pair of sunshades as Mona drove like a bat out of hell. Like Simone, Mona was hardly recognizable, donning a bob style wig and a maroon sundress as her own disguise.

"Yeah, he sure did. Thank God for him."

"Thank God for all the people you've loved before, right?" Simone cackled as Mona grimaced.

"Jees. That's certainly one way to look at it." Mona had called Lyle, who owned La Cocina, early that morning and explained why she needed to get rid of a couple of cops who were assigned to protect her. To her relief, he had immediately been game to help, arranging for a change of clothes, transportation, and just enough confusion to facilitate their escape without completely disrupting his customers' lunch breaks. The plan was that Mona would take Sophie to the bathroom under the guise of nature's call. Before entering the stall nearest a small window, one of the waitresses handed Mona her current disguise and Lyle's car keys. Dressed in her new getup, Mona had easily walked out of the restroom unrecognized in the crowd, leaving Sophie with the waitress inside the restroom. She had then stridden unnoticed past the cop watching Simone and out of the restaurant, expecting to be stopped at any moment, but no one came after her. Once Mona had been in the clear, the waitress had dropped Sophie out of the restroom window into the waiting arms of Simone, who had by then exited La Cocina via the kitchen back door to claim the child. The Range Rover had been parked in back of the restaurant, giving Mona just enough time to locate it, fire up the engine, and burn rubber out of the parking lot after picking up Simone and Sophie near the restroom window. "I feel so unworthy, ya know. I don't deserve his help after the way I treated him. God." Mona had mercilessly dumped Lyle only a few months ago and hardly been receptive to his frequent calls since then. For some reason, however, he had never developed any malicious feelings toward her, a paradox that she had reasoned was due to his ego since his unmitigated pursuit of reconciliation had reeked of his refusal to accept rejection. Now that he had so willingly helped her and her family, however, she was forced to reconsider his possible motives. And what so far occurred to her – that perhaps he had actually cared – made her feel like something less than crud. Apparently, neither Lyle nor Jocelyn had deserved to cross her pitiless path.

"Mom, where are we going?" Sophie was now wearing a baseball cap to make her look more boyish. Anyone who inspected her, however, would have thought the child was somewhat odd since she was still clutching her President Barbie doll to her chest. Sophie had been told that today's events were just a cloak and dagger type of adventure that Aunt Simone had concocted as a way to have fun with her great niece. Neither Simone nor Mona reminded the child that she had forgotten to suck her thumb so far today in all the excitement.

"We're going to Galveston, baby. Doesn't that sound like fun?" Mona did her best to sound enthused for Sophie's benefit.

"Yeeessss! Are we going to the beach?"

"We just might. Let's play it by ear, okay?"

"Okay!"

Simone caught Mona's eye. They were both relieved to see Sophie slowly emerging from her embattled psyche.

"Toots will be expecting us to arrive by 2:00. Think we'll make it?" Simone buckled her seatbelt as she spoke.

"I think Toots will be seeing us sooner than 2:00." Mona activated the police radar and then stomped her foot down on the accelerator pedal, taking the car to ninety miles per hour. Just then, her cell phone rang. "Right on time," she remarked as she glanced at the caller ID screen. Unsurprisingly, it was Harold. She pressed a button that directed the call to her voice mail box and then dialed Richard to let him know that she would be out of pocket for a couple of days. When he questioned her current plans and her whereabouts, she remained vague and told him to let Harold know he'd hear from her early next week. Mona could tell that Richard was displeased with her ambiguity, but after a few minutes of fruitless grilling, he relented, powerless to persuade her to provide more information.

"That guy just doesn't give up, does he?" Simone commented on Richard's persistent questioning once Mona ended the call with him.

"He's just doing his job. The cops want to know where I am so he's required to ask. There's nothing he can do if I don't tell him, though."

"Didn't you say that he's one of Aaron's attorneys?"

"He used to be, but I doubt that he is now. It would be a conflict of interest, wouldn't it?"

"Still, I don't like the guy. I think you should get someone else."

"And I think you're being paranoid."

"Paranoia can be good sometimes."

"I agree, but in the long run it really doesn't matter, does it?"

Simone frowned. "No, I guess it doesn't."

—⁘—

Within forty-five minutes, Mona had crossed the Galveston city line and the coastline, which Mona had not seen since she was a very young girl, was now in full view. The scenery evoked pleasant memories despite the danger that had brought her here. Since they had a little time to spare before Simone's friend, Toots, would be expecting them, Mona decided to stop at a Gap store located in a shopping strip near the beach. It was time to get those blue jeans she had been wanting for the past few days. She also planned to buy a pair of tennis shoes, having donated her last unworn pair to charity at least six years ago. She could remember a time when jeans and tennis shoes had been her standard apparel choice. But that had been before Aaron, before Mrs. Baker had come into being, before she had sort of lost herself in her pursuit of a new identity.

"I like these." Simone held a pair of jeans against her body. "What do ya think?"

Mona quickly checked out the jeans. "They're cute. You gonna get 'em?" She was holding around five pairs of jeans that she had quickly selected after verifying their sizes. She was going to buy them without trying them on.

"Nah, I've got plenty of clothes at my beach house. I don't need any more jeans, that's for sure." Simone placed the jeans back on the rack. "I think I'm going to take Sophie next door for some clothes since we left all her stuff in the Mercedes."

"Okay, make it fast. Pick out what she needs and I'll be over to pay for it in a few minutes."

"Girl, I got this! You're not the only one of us with cash on 'em." She grabbed Sophie's hand and smiled down at her. The two then left the store.

In that instant, something overwhelmed Mona. It was a feeling that she had not expected and that she was surprised to be experiencing at this particular moment:

joy. She loved Simone dearly. What a joy to have her sister back after so many years of separation. Within just a few days, they had fallen into a comfortable relationship that belied the fact that they had not seen each other or spoken in nearly a decade. And Mona could feel qualities of her old self returning now, qualities that she felt ashamed to have brushed aside after getting married. And there was something else – she was beginning to like herself again. She hadn't realized that she had ever stopped liking herself, but Simone must have been right yet again. A warm feeling was glowing inside Mona today and it was brought about by her sister's presence and her strength.

Mona used a few more minutes to collect additional items that caught her eye, mostly t-shirts of various colors and shorts. She then spotted a modest pair of white tennis shoes to finish off her rapid spree, paid for all the clothes, and rushed next door. Before she could get inside the store, however, Simone walked out with an ecstatic Sophie, who had been allowed five minutes to pick out anything she wanted. As it turned out, most of the clothes that Simone had wound up purchasing for the girl were the child's favorite color – green.

"Good God!" Mona cringed when she looked inside the bag.

"What's wrong, Mommy?" Sophie was giddy beyond words.

"Nothing's wrong with her, sweetie," Simone broke in as they walked to the Range Rover and opened the doors. "You've got terrific taste like your aunt." They all got into the car, Sophie smiling from ear to ear as Mona sighed with her hand on her forehead before starting the engine.

"For God's sake, you could have picked out at least one pair of blue pants or maybe one orange blouse for her."

"Hey! As long as I'm buyin', she can have whatever she wants. That's what aunts are for. Now go to the red light and turn left. We should just make it to Toots's condo before she gets worried."

—⁂—

It was a few minutes before two o'clock when the sisters took an elevator up to Toots's condo, which was located in a high-rise building overlooking the ocean. The building was old, but well-kept and remodeled inside, appearing to be populated by retirees for the most part. There were several other condo buildings located nearby, all with fantastic views of the coastline and Mona suddenly wished she could just disappear inside one of the condo units with Sophie and Simone. She wished that she could escape all the drama and jeopardy that lately hounded her every footstep, never to be seen again. But it just wasn't possible. Simone had a life that she was eager to start as a social worker, a future that Mona would never want to snatch away from her sister. It would be easy enough for her and Sophie to vanish in a crowd somewhere, but it would also destroy Simone's dreams. So Mona let the idea go, ousting it from her mind before she could discover a yearning to cling to the notion.

Toots, one of Simone's closest friends who also happened to be a stripper, lived on the sixteenth floor of the condo complex. Mona didn't know what to expect when Simone knocked on the woman's door, but what she saw standing in the doorway was far, far beyond her wildest imaginations.

"Hey, girl! It's about time you got here!" Toots was the color of a chocolate brownie and stood over six feet tall. She was skinnier than the wispiest top models on magazine covers these days, extravagantly made up with long fake eyelashes that were practically encrusted with mascara, and wearing the tightest pair of glitter pants that Mona had ever seen in her life. The woman's breasts were bulging so far out beyond the rest of her body that they could have doubled as a tabletop. Essentially, she looked like a rock on toothpicks. "Get on in here!" She pulled Simone into her condo and held the door open as Mona and Sophie followed in flabbergasted awe of Toots's appearance. "Well, now you must be Mona. Simone has told me all about you and let me say right now that the pleasure is all mine, okay?" She shook Mona's hand with a very limp grip.

"Thank you, Toots. I'm glad to meet you as well. Under the circumstances, I'm really glad that you've let us come here."

"Honey, please! Let me tell you somethin'. I have known your sister for almost ten years, ya hear me? Ten years! And I believe in my heart that she is good people, okay? The best. She's been a good friend to me and I am honored to return the favor." She leaned down to face

Sophie. "Miss Sophie, I am pleased to make your acquaintance as well."

Sophie blushed and shook Toots's hand. "Thank you, Miss Toots."

"You and me are going to be good friends, okay?" Toots rubbed the top of Sophie's head.

"Okay." Sophie blushed again and buried her head in Mona's abdomen.

"I see that you've got a new wig." Simone touched the flamboyantly golden hair on Toots's head.

Toots immediately began to primp. "You like it, girl? It's gonna drive those white men crazy when I wear it for my show! You know how they love me!"

"Yep, I'm sure you're right." Simone managed to respond without expressing an opinion on Toots's grandiosity.

"You know it!" Toots shepherded her guests into the living room area. To Mona's surprise, the condo was a very comfortable size, she guessed around three-thousand square feet at the very least. Toots had decorated the living room in conservative shades of beige and tan, another surprise given the woman's absurdly overstated appearance. "Now, is anyone hungry? If so, just say the word and we'll get somethin' delivered from somewhere on my dime."

"I'm not hungry. We all ate a few hours ago." Mona didn't want to walk in asking more of Toots than what Toots had already graciously agreed to do for her.

"Mommy, I want some water." Sophie had thought she was whispering, but Toots easily heard the girl.

"Water comin' up! Anything else, honey?"

Sophie blushed again as soon as she realized that she had Toots's attention. "No, ma'am."

"Are you sure? You don't need to be shy with Toots, okay?"

Mona was beginning to realize that the word "okay" was going to be incorporated into a disproportionate amount of Toots's sentences.

"Okay." Sophie's blush deepened as Toots immediately scampered from the room with an exaggerated twist of her hips.

"I know she's a little over the top," Simone said after Toots was out of earshot, "but she is sweeter than syrup. And I'd trust her with my life if push came to shove."

"If you trust her, then I trust her. Your opinion is good enough for me."

"Okay, baby," Toots hustled back into the room, "here's your water."

Sophie took the glass and began drinking the cold contents.

"What do you say to Toots, Sophie?"

Sophie swallowed quickly. "Thank you, Miss Toots."

"You're welcome!" She looked from Mona to Simone. "You two really don't want anything, huh?"

"No, we're fine," Simone leaned back into the sofa as Toots daintily took a seat beside her. "Toots, have you ever heard of a Columbian drug family called the Escobars?"

"Ooh, honey, yes!" She sat up straight and batted her eyelashes. "And you have, too!"

"See, that's why I'm askin' because I know I've heard of 'em, but I don't remember when or why."

"Girl, the Escobars were the ones behind Lola and her family gettin' killed last year." Lola had been a prostitute with a severely debilitating drug habit. Since Simone had always avoided mingling with addicts, they had only crossed paths a few times over the years.

"Oh, God, that's right." Simone's hand flew to her cheek as Mona gasped and leaned toward Sophie.

"Honey, why don't you go into Miss Toots's bedroom and watch TV while we talk about grown-up stuff?" Mona's eyes then beseeched Toots. "Do you mind?"

"Of course I don't mind!" Toots flapped a hand in the air and stood up again. "Come on, baby. Let's find something you'll like to watch." She left the room with Sophie awkwardly trailing behind her while looking over her shoulder at Mona.

"It's okay, sweetie. I'll come get you in a little while." Mona tried to smile, but the effort was especially strained now that Toots had shared her personal knowledge of the grisly enemy Mona was up against.

"Mona, there is no way we want the Escobars to think you're tryin' to bring down their drug business," Simone immediately cautioned. "We've gotta get on with our plan as quickly as possible. Otherwise, you're dead, maybe me, too. Ain't no doubt in my mind about that."

Mona breathed heavily and frowned at the floor. "I know you're right, but I still hate it. Yes, it needs to be done so all of this can just be over, but that doesn't make it easy."

"I've told you before – it ain't never easy to play God, but sometimes it's necessary." Simone's voice had resumed resolution and calm.

"Yeah, honey," Toots hastily sashayed back in with all the grace of a Southern belle. Mona couldn't help noting that her carriage was in utter defiance of the flamboyant apparel that showcased her breasts and bony legs. If not for her breasts, Toots's body fat ratio would have been flat zero. "Those Escobars ain't nothin' nice, ya hear me? Nothin' nice." She returned to her seat beside Simone. "Ole Lola was a sweet thang that just got mixed up with the wrong crowd, got turned out by that sorry pimp of hers so he could keep her on the streets, okay? But he didn't count on her stealin' the stash that he was supposed to be sellin' and those Escobars don't take kindly to their money goin' up somebody's nose instead of in their pockets." Toots crossed her legs and relaxed against the sofa cushions facing Simone. "I would say to Lola all the time, 'Lola, girl, you got to stop this thang you're doin', okay? You got to get yourself clean before somebody kills you or your children.' But she was just too strung out to think straight! And, of course, I didn't know that she had started stealin' the drugs because no one would even pay her to go down on 'em, ya know. She looked bad, honey, okay? Toe up from the flo up, okay?"

"So the Escobars killed her for using their drugs without paying for them." Mona was appalled by the story, but not surprised by the results after what she'd seen growing up.

"Uh huh, that's what I heard, girl. Killed her, her pimp, and both of her kids last year. Paid somebody to shoot 'em all at their house to send a message to anyone else who might be thinkin' about jackin' with them, okay? And I'm pretty sure that everybody heard that message, honey."

Mona looked at Simone. "Well, that explains why Aaron is trying to make sure everybody knows that he's been set up. If the Escobars got the impression that he was trying to steal from them, he wouldn't be safe anywhere on the planet."

"They may already have that impression for all we know."

"Good Lord! Is your husband mixed up with the Escobars?" Toots's posture straightened with shock.

"That's what it sounds like."

"Oh, honey, that's bad. That's real bad." She leapt up and went to a window to close the blinds and draw the curtains. "That's awful!"

"You don't have to worry, Toots, nobody knows we're here. We were very careful when we left Houston." Simone watched her friend go to the other three windows in the living room to shut off visibility.

"And we're gonna keep it that way, okay?"

Somebody knocked on Toots's door, causing all three women to nearly hit the ceiling before Toots caught her breath. "That's probably just Mr. Cooper. He's always tryin' to flirt. Comes down to the club to see my show every week. Hold on." Toots went to the door as Mona and Simone looked on with their breaths still caught in their throats. "Who is it?" She looked through the peephole on the door. A muffled voice responded from the other side of the door. "I'm sorry, sir, but you've got the wrong residence. You might want to try another floor." She continued to look through the peephole as she spoke. "Alright now. You have a good day, honey." She remained still as a statue at the peephole as the visitor walked away from the door.

"Who was that?" Simone called from the living room.

Toots finally turned around and came back to the sofa. "I don't know, but he sho wasn't gettin' in, okay?"

Both Mona and Simone exhaled simultaneously and looked at each other. "Maybe we should leave," Simone stated. "I don't want to bring trouble to your doorstep."

"Honey, no! I won't hear of it. It's all good, nobody's comin' here. You said you were careful and I'm sure you were." Toots turned to Mona. "You can go ahead and leave your little girl here, okay? She'll be safe with me. I don't know if Simone told you, but I've got skills with a gun. If somebody tries to jack with me or Sophie while you're gone, I'll bust a cap in his ass. Us street girls don't play, okay?"

Mona nodded her head and looked at Simone again. "You're right, Toots. We don't play, do we?"

—⁓—

A couple of hours later, Simone decided to take the Range Rover to her beach house while Mona and Sophie took a nap. Simone needed to collect some more clothes since her bags had been left in the Mercedes along with Sophie's and Mona's. She and Mona had considered staying at her beach house overnight, but thought better of it just in case the cops decided to drive by the place at some point. Not only did Toots's condo seem like a better option, but it gave Sophie a chance to get a little comfortable with Toots before being left alone with the woman tomorrow. Mona was planning to leave Sophie with Toots so she and Simone could carry out the rest of their plan without worrying about Sophie's safety.

Simone walked out into the sunshine, got into the car, and looked around at everything and everyone. Multiple beachgoers were walking along the wide, concrete sidewalks that lined the upper part of the shore for several miles along with various specialty tourist shops and clothing stores. Simone's beach house wasn't too far away and she was fairly certain that no one was watching her at this moment. She would be careful about approaching the beach house, however, since the cops knew where she actually lived and could easily have set up a stakeout by now in the off chance of locating Mona.

Simone drove slowly down the street, stopping at every yellow light long before they were set to turn red. If anyone was following her, it would look awfully suspicious for that person to also stop rather than speeding through the yellow light as most people were prone to do. So far, no one stopped except her so she proceeded with her drive to the beach house.

Galveston was pretty cool. The breeze coming off the ocean blew right through the car's open windows, bringing bits of sand with it. She could feel the grit on her skin when she ran her hand over her face. Nice. Once she had hated the grit, but now she appreciated it because she had been missing her home, her space. There was very little traffic on the road with her as she turned down the street that would take her to the beach house she loved so well. Not that it was elaborate or anything, but it was peaceful. Everything about it made her feel good to be in her skin.

A few blocks away from the beach house, Simone stopped the car and stared straight ahead at all the surroundings. Nothing looked out of place, no suspect cars around, no people hanging out nearby that she'd never seen before. Everything looked normal so she drove forward and soon parked in front of the house. Home sweet home.

After unlocking her front door and entering the house, Simone first spent a few minutes looking out the large windows that faced the ocean. This was her favorite spot in the house. The white foam cresting the waves always looked so inviting that a part of her mind would launch itself into the sea, into the mists of serenity. After being stung by jellyfish a few years ago, she had tired of actually swimming in the ocean, but that didn't stop her imagination from taking her there from this window. But there was no time for an extended fantasy right now. She needed to get the clothes she'd come for and get out. No reason for her to gamble by staying longer than necessary.

Simone turned her back on the view and quickly went upstairs to her bedroom. As with her apartment in League City, the place was fastidiously neat. The original hardwood floors that had been installed when the house was built decades ago were still intact, highly polished, and in excellent condition. Her queen-size bed was the prize, though. The mattresses were so comfortable that they may as well have been clouds. She could hardly feel them beneath her body when she slept on them. Simone forced herself to pass the bed in favor of accomplishing her solitary objective – clothing.

Around twenty minutes later, Simone was standing outside the beach house with a duffle bag of clothes that would support her needs for the next two days or so. She preferred to travel light. If she needed anything more, she'd just have to buy it.

Once situated in the Range Rover again, she started the engine and let it idle for a short time while she looked in the rearview mirror, stared out the windows in every direction, and turned on the radio. Everything still looked normal. Good.

She shifted the car into drive and headed back to Toots's condo. When she crossed the first busy intersection leading from her beach house, however, she failed to notice the silver Mazda Miata that turned onto the street and began to unobtrusively follow her.

TEN

The drive back to Toots's condo was shorter than Simone would have preferred, affording her no time alone to think. She decided to take a detour that would put her on the beachfront, where she parked the car in a spot along the coastline. She then perched herself squarely in the brilliant sunlight on the car hood facing the water and watched beachgoers perform their various activities – constructing sandcastles, surfing, frolicking in the shallowest waters, tossing up stale bread to seagulls gliding through the sky. There was even a game of beach volleyball underway several yards from her parking place, a group of women versus some men.

Everything looked so normal, so ordinary even as Simone's world was threatening to collapse around her. But she had beaten the odds before, a reality that she now clung to for continued sustenance. Certainly, she was scarred, but alive and victorious, filled with a sureness that she was mentally equipped to handle anything that life could throw at her. She was a modern day gladiator, her weapon of choice: any gun she could get her hands on. It occurred to her that maybe her child-hood had been preparing her for this very moment in time when she would be instrumental in saving Mona's life. God only knew what may have happened by now if Simone hadn't been forced onto the streets, thrust into a life that compelled her to learn how to defend herself. Thanks to the very circumstances that had embittered her toward Beatrice – Simone didn't call her Mama anymore – she had been able to preserve her sister's existence. And there was also little Sophie, of course, a lovable little girl who was a few years younger than the child that Simone could have had when she was a stupid teenager making all the wrong decisions about boys. If Beatrice had known about Simone's secret sex life, the world really would have caved in on her!

It was a fate that Simone had barely escaped, but never forgotten and absolutely never spoke about to anyone. While in the ninth grade, she had developed a crush on one of the school's star football players, Tyrone, a real stud who enjoyed his popularity with the girls. And since he was a senior, he was all the more enticing to young idiots like Simone, who were eager to believe almost anything a boy told them. Despite all of Beatrice's warnings about men and boys, Simone had thought her mother had gotten it all wrong because Tyrone was definitely different. And when he professed his undying love, she had bought it with all her foolish heart, soon afterward letting him have his way in an untamed field near the school when they both skipped classes. They had gone on this way for several weeks, falling into a routine that required an increasingly creative list of pretexts to be briefly excused from classes until Simone had stumbled onto the truth – Tyrone was pulling the same crap with several of her classmates, all of whom were equally as gullible as she had been. Unfortunately, Simone had also figured out that she was pregnant, a disaster that precluded her heartache in favor of her fear of death because Beatrice was sure to kill her. Simone had heard all the warnings throughout her life so she knew what personal harm and perhaps even homelessness that awaited her if the truth came out. Having a baby was not an option. Period.

Suddenly confronted with her own mortality, Simone was much too consumed with her fear of Beatrice to quake indefinitely at Tyrone's betrayal. Instead, she had desperately set about finding a way to end the pregnancy as quickly and quietly as possible. At age fourteen, she obviously had no money of her own nor did she know anyone other than crack dealers who did. So she had seen no other choice but to turn to the only adult who she thought she could trust: Uncle Clarence. To her relief, Simone had rightfully assumed that he would be willing to help her and, more importantly, to keep her secret from Beatrice. What Simone had not counted on was that his confidence would come at an extremely high price, providing him with an opening to act on sick impulses that utterly destroyed her teenage years. Yes, he had kept Simone's secret and eventually helped her to obtain birth control pills, but she could not have guessed at the time that his own selfish motives had also been at work. Looking back on it all now, she remembered the smirk that had been pasted on his face at the clinic when she had gotten the pills. It was all so clear in hindsight. God! Her whole life had been ruined because of her inability to discern wolves in sheep's clothing before they could inflict their damage. And her malfunctioning wolf radar had altogether broken down yet again when she had married a rotten con artist who posed as a perfect gentleman but turned out to be quite the opposite, relieving his stress on her head, her stomach, her back, and any other place on her body that he could punch. Luckily for him, she had decided to leave rather than allowing his last swing to be at the barrel of her gun.

And so here she was now, sitting on the hood of this Range Rover, single by choice and necessity for sanity, puzzled at how normal the world seemed despite her current lot in life. Still, she could not overlook the fact that Galveston had been pretty good to her. She had entered the city as a teenage runaway with nothing. Now she had made a life here and was positioned to start doing some real good by helping troubled youths in need of meaningful guidance. She would tell them to learn how to rely on themselves, to trust themselves, and to lead honest lives. The world didn't have to be a walk through hell, but it was bound to be for sycophants, codependents, criminals, and self-proclaimed victims who chose not to overcome their adversities. "Choose your friends wisely," Simone would tell them. "Don't allow people you can't trust to occupy your precious life space." As for Simone's friends, she could count on both hands the number of people that she trusted and all of them were women of the night, either hookers or strippers. Like

Beatrice had said so many years ago, you couldn't believe a damned thing that a man said so save yourself the trouble of trying. Beatrice's truth had turned out to be Simone's truth as well. Perhaps Simone's attitude would change one day, but it was going to take a very special, patient man – if she lived long enough. For now, however, Simone was on a hiatus from all men largely because she simply didn't trust her lackluster track record.

"Heaven! I thought that was you!" A petite, deeply tanned blonde woman with beach ball breasts and a nearly nonexistent red bikini approached from the beachfront. She went by the stage name Scarlet, so chosen because red was her favorite color. Scarlet had once worked at the same strip joint where Simone had started out and may not have heard that Simone had quit the business. Heaven had been Simone's stage name.

"What's up, Scarlet?" Simone smiled modestly to appear friendly although she didn't feel like being bothered. Until the woman had been mere footsteps away, Simone hadn't even noticed her advance. "I answer to my Christian name now so just call me Simone."

"Ooh! So you're not strippin' no more?" She cheesed her ultra-white teeth for Simone.

"No, I've given it up to become a social worker. I graduated from college last year."

"That's so nice. It really is. 'Course, I don't see how you can give up all the money we make for a pauper's take, but to each his own, ya know?"

"My words exactly. So how are things?"

"Good, good. I think I'm gonna have to get rid of Terrance, though. Caught him cheatin' on me again with one of the other girls. He says that he's sorry and all, but I don't know."

"You caught him cheatin' and you just think you need to get rid of him? Girl, he would already be history if he was my man."

"Yeah, but that's why you don't have one, right?" Scarlet laughed half-heartedly. "I mean, all men cheat so you'll never keep one if you expect him to be faithful. I just ask that the man be discreet, know what I'm sayin'? If he's gonna cheat, don't be stupid enough to get caught. I guarantee you that he wouldn't catch me." Now she grinned sheepishly.

"Well, sounds like another case of to each his own. Personally, I'd rather be single than put up with a lyin' bastard."

"I hear you, girlfriend." Her eyes roamed the scenery before finally resting on a place behind Simone's shoulder. "You thinkin' about givin' anyone a chance in the near future?"

"Why?"

"'Cause you definitely got an admirer at twelve o'clock."

Simone turned her head a full half-circle to look behind her. Sure enough there was a Hispanic man leaning against a Mazda Miata parked a respectable distance away, but certainly within plain sight.

"Until you turned your head, he was just starin' at you."

"How do ya know he wasn't starin' at you? Hispanic men have a thing for blondes, ya know."

"I know he likes you because he was starin' at you before I came up to ya. That's how I know. Maybe he likes his women exotic." Scarlet winked and smiled broadly again. "Want me to wave him over?"

"Hell no!" Simone leapt off the car and walked around to the driver side window, which was fully down. "Listen, I think you should get outta here. That guy looks like bad news and you don't need to be seen talkin' to me right now." Simone leaned into the car to grab her purse. She had a cell phone in it somewhere.

"What, are you in some kind of trouble?"

Simone located the cell phone and pressed a button to switch the power on as she spoke. "Just get outta here, alright? I'll tell you about it later." She opened the car door and got in, already dialing Toots's phone number at the condo.

Scarlet lingered near the car with apparent concern. "Anything I can do to help?"

"Not unless you wanna get killed. Now get outta here, okay?"

Now Scarlet looked shocked. "Are you serious?"

"Go!"

"Well...okay...Call me in a coupla days. Or I'll call you to check in, make sure you're alright." Scarlet slowly began to edge away, walking backwards while awaiting Simone's response.

"Yeah, okay, fine." Just then, Toots was on the line so Simone's attention was pulled entirely away as Scarlet continued down the beach. "Hey! Got some bad news." Simone started the car engine. "I think some shit is about to go down and I need your help."

"You got it, girl. Just tell me what to do."

—⁓—

Simone meandered down a few streets in the Range Rover, appearing to have no specific destination as she occasionally stopped at a few small shops. The idea was to buy some time for Toots to get in position while allowing the imbecile shadowing her to think that he had not been made. As she glanced in her rearview mirror to confirm his continued pursuit, Simone scolded herself for failing to notice him earlier. He hung back a safe distance, but his audacity – following her in nearly empty streets – smacked of either desperation or stupidity. Clearly, she wasn't the target or he would have killed her by now. No telling how long he had been tailing her, but he obviously hoped to be led to Mona.

"Asshole," Simone cursed aloud. She wondered how many associates he may already have told about locating her. He may only be a drone, tasked to keep her in sight until the real deal arrived. Didn't seem to be a cop so that left a possible connection to the Escobars.

After driving around aimlessly for over half an hour, Simone finally made her way to the high-rise condo complex where Toots would be waiting. She parked the car, grabbed her duffle bag, and began walking toward the building entrance, fully expecting that her stalker would be forced to follow her inside since he could easily lose her in such a large building. Minutes later, he rushed into the lobby where Simone was awaiting the elevator. As he drew nearer, Simone instinctively tensed, but smiled nonchalantly. He wordlessly returned the smile as the elevator doors slid open. Once again, as she expected, he had no choice but to step into the elevator with her, whereupon he made a chivalrous show of insisting that she select her floor before he did on the solitary number pad in the elevator. After Simone selected floor twenty-two, he selected twenty-four and then stepped back, allowing her a polite amount of space. Simone considered the grim possibility that he might be planning to exit the elevator with her and put a gun to her head or back so she would lead him to her sister. This setup seemed likely.

Now trapped inside the tiny compartment with a potential killer, Simone's mind raced with the various scenarios under which he could murder her and get away. She knew that she wasn't being logical, though, because – as she noted earlier – she would already be dead if she were the target. She tried not to fidget as the elevator crept upward at an impossibly slow rate. Simone could swear that beads of sweat were forming on her forehead, but she refused to reach up and wipe her skin. Certainly, her palms were clammy beyond all reason as she fought against her desire to whip around with her gun pointed at the face of the man standing so boldly behind her. She compromised with herself and bit into her lower lip instead.

Finally, the doors opened at floor twenty-two and Simone stepped off the elevator. Before the man could make a move, however, Toots stepped into his line of sight with the barrel of her large, silencer-equipped Magnum pointed directly at his forehead. To keep the elevator doors open, she also inserted her foot against one of the steel doors. Were it not for the spectacle of seeing a black, blonde Amazon stripper in sparkling hotpants handling a gun with expert confidence, any onlooker's gaze would have been glued to that skeletal leg for fear that the elevator doors would snap forward and altogether break it off.

"I'll bet that you're surprised, aren't you?" Toots's voice was deadly serious as Simone appeared behind her with her own gun drawn. "You weren't expectin' to see no big black woman pointin' a big black gun at you, huh, sugar?"

The guy's eyes were suddenly wide open and his hands held up. "¡Perdóname! Lo siento. ¡No habla inglés, señora!"

Toots confusedly looked at Simone, who kept her eyes and gun trained on their captive. "What did he just say?"

"He said that he doesn't speak English, which is a damned lie because he was talkin' when we got on the elevator."

"Oh, okay, it's like that." She raised an eyebrow and overtly released the safety on the gun. When she next spoke, there was a marked amount of incense in her voice. "If there's one thing I can't stand, it's a lyin' sack of dog crap like yourself, okay? You got one more chance to behave before I shoot you somewhere that I know you won't be happy about. Got me?" She paused while maintaining eye contact. "Now. Kindly step off this el-evator." Toots waved her gun toward the hallway.

Still speechless, the man slowly slunk out, at which point Toots removed her foot, allowing the doors to ease closed.

"That's real good. Now walk in front of me down the hall. We're going to unit 22D just up that way." The man stared from Simone to Toots without moving. The fear in his eyes was acute as he absorbed the reality that he had been set up. "Go on. Move. Chop-chop. Or I could shoot you right here. Makes no difference to me, okay? Seein' as how you been conspirin' to kill a friend of mine."

"You don't understand!" The man's speech was thick with a Spanish accent.

"Well, you can explain it all when we get inside 22D. Now start walkin'."

—⚡—

Toots's friend, Mr. Cooper, owned several condo units near the coastline that he rented out. Currently, one of those units – 22D – was unoccupied and located several blocks from Toots's residence, where Mona and Sophie still slept in blissful ignorance of the current developments. It was a perfect spot to ambush the drone, who was now strapped to a chair inside the condo and sweating profusely.

"So why are you followin' me?" Simone asked the most obvious question first.

"To keep an eye on you, das all." His eyes darted to Toots, who still kept her gun trained on him, though now his groin, not his head, was in the crosshairs. "I swear!"

"Followin' me for who? And why?"

"I don't know!"

"What do you mean you don't know?"

"I jus following orders!"

"Whose orders?"

"I don't know!"

"He sho don't know a lot, does he? I think we should just shoot him. At least we'll keep him from telling his buddies anything."

"You ain't gonna shoot me, bitch!" The man's facial expression had abruptly transformed from meek to sinister as both Toots and Simone reacted with stunned silence at the personality change. "If something happen to me, you and your whole family are dead." He smiled evilly, allowing the full measure of his ruthlessness to be revealed. Of course, it could have been an act to throw the women off the stench of his fright. Both Simone and Toots had seen his macho type too many times to count.

The gun went off and the man wailed at the top of his lungs as Toots now smiled wickedly and Simone reflexively flinched. "As you can see from the bullet hole in your foot, Mr. Shit for Brains, I ain't buyin' your act, okay? Consider that a warnin' of what's to come if you don't start answerin' my friend's questions. My PMS is your worst enemy right now, okay?"

"You crazy bitch!" He finally yelled between grunts of pain. "I'm gonna git you for dees!"

Toots promptly shot the man in his other foot.

"Auuugh!" He roared uncontrollably again. "¡Me ayuda! ¡Me ayuda!"

"Nobody is gonna help you, dickwad," Simone stated coldly. "This is an old buildin' and the walls are nice and thick. Yell all you want, but nobody will hear you."

"That's right. Do you really think we would have lured you somewhere that you could get away without talkin' first? Give us some credit for brains, okay?"

The man was dripping with sweat, his mouth hanging open as he lowered his chin to his chest with defeat. Both Simone and Toots could hear that his breathing had become labored and Simone deduced that he might be going into shock.

"Hey, you okay? Or do you want us to go ahead and put you out of your misery?" Simone had no sympathy for him whatsoever. Before their arrival, Toots had placed a large plastic sheath beneath and around the man's chair so the threat of his death would be obvious. The plastic also ensured that no blood got on the carpet. Neither woman wanted to kill their captive, but both were prepared to do so if necessary. Should he be killed, they would simply roll his body in the plastic and call one of their other street buddies to come get the body. It was all good.

"Just shoot me," the man finally panted. "I dead anyway if I answer your questions."

Toots looked at Simone. "Better hurry up. I'm sure he called somebody before he came into the buildin'. We need to get outta here in a few minutes."

"You're right." Simone maintained a distance several feet from the man. "All I wanna know is who sent you, the cops or the Escobars."

"Cops?" The man spat at Simone's feet. "I ain't talkin' to no stinkin' cops, chocha." He sneered menacingly.

"So that just leaves the Escobars." Simone knowingly looked at Toots as an understanding of the danger confronting Mona yet again racked her mind.

"Hold up," Toots interjected. "What does chocha mean?"

"He just called me a pussycat, but without the cat part." Preoccupied, Simone didn't care about the insult, but Toots didn't take it so well. She immediately shot the man in his knee.

"¡Madre de Dios!" He threw his head back and screamed at the ceiling before finally losing consciousness.

"Thanks a lot, Toots." Simone went over to the man and felt his pulse on his neck. "Out cold. Now I can't find out how many of his friends are probably outside waitin' for us."

"Honey, that don't matter, okay? I got your back." She walked into the kitchen and came back with the wig that Simone had worn when she and Mona had ditched the cops in Houston. "No one is lookin' for me so don't worry about that. And with this wig on you, no one will know who you are, okay?"

Simone unceremoniously accepted the wig from Toots. "What about him?" She placed the wig on her head and stripped down to her underwear, a matching pink panty and bra set made from spandex, which meant it could easily pass for a common skimpy bathing suit. The idea was to put more attention on her comely figure than on her face should she catch anyone's attention while exiting the building.

"I'm just gonna send Eddie over here for him, tell him we got a cleanup job. He'll handle it for us." Eddie was a muscle-bound bouncer at the strip joint where Simone and Toots had met years ago.

"That'll work." Simone crammed her clothes into the duffle bag she had brought inside with her before turning to face Toots again. "So how do I look?"

"Like a regular ho, okay?"

"Good." She tossed her purse over her shoulder and held her duffle bag out for Toots to take. "I'll meet you back at your place in around an hour. That gives me enough time to make sure I'm not tailed."

"Not so fast. We got one more thing to do." Toots went over to the man and dug through all his pockets, locating his wallet and cell phone. She immediately tossed the cell phone to Simone and then pulled his driver's license from his wallet as Simone accessed the man's personal phone directory. "Well looka here, looka here. Our man is named Antonio Pollizi."

"Isn't Pollizi an Italian name?" Simone was now scrolling through the incoming and outgoing call screens since the cell phone directory had been empty.

Toots shrugged nonchalantly. "I guess. Maybe he's both Italian and Mexican, which makes him really hot to trot, okay?" She looked more closely at his face. "Now that I look at him, his nose does look a little funny for a Hispanic."

"Give me a break. The name is probably just as fake as his driver's license." Simone finally sighed, turned off the cell phone, and tossed it into her purse. "I don't recognize any of the phone numbers in his cell, not that I expected to. I'm pretty sure that the phone is a throw-away, but I'll hold on to it in case it comes in handy later."

Toots now held up a wad of money and smiled. "Good news. Antonio is buyin' us dinner tonight."

ELEVEN

By the time Simone got back to Toots's condo, her friend had given Mona the full lowdown of the most recent events while Sophie was instructed to again watch television in another room out of earshot. The condo was filled with the scent of Mexican food when Simone entered, now clothed in a cheap pair of shorts and a t-shirt to cover her underwear.

"Thank God you made it back!" Mona rushed to her sister at the door and hugged her. "I can't bear the idea of losing you again so soon after getting you back."

"Don't worry about me, sis. I can take care of myself." Simone returned Mona's hug and then reached to her head to remove the wig of braids.

"I see that you got some new digs," Toots commented on Simone's clothes.

"Yeah, I walked to the nearest thrift shop after leaving Antonio and then caught a cab."

"A cab? Why would you do that?" Mona was puzzled as well as concerned that their only transportation, the

Range Rover, was now ditched somewhere. Lyle would not be pleased to hear about this.

"Had to. We have to assume that Antonio told his friends what I was drivin' when he was followin' me."

"That's right," Toots piped in. "Good thinking."

"I can only hope that he was too dumb to give the license plate to anyone. He just needed to keep me in sight and hope that I would lead him to you."

"Oh," Mona nodded soberly. "I see."

"In fact, I wouldn't be surprised if there's somebody watchin' the car right now." Simone looked at Toots as a new thought popped into her mind. "Did you call Eddie yet?"

"You know it. Why?"

"I'm thinkin' we should ask him to get the Range Rover in a day or two when things cool off."

"I'll call him again right now." Toots went for her phone in the kitchen.

"Wait!" Another thought occurred to Simone. "He won't have the keys."

"And?" Toots shrugged.

"You're right. He won't need keys." She looked at Mona with visible relief as Toots left to make the call. "Eddie is a godsend. He's as big as a gorilla and very protective of the girls he guards at the club. And if anyone tries any kind of bullshit with him, they won't know what hit 'em."

"Is he going to kill Antonio?" Mona was mortified at this possible eventuality.

"No!" Simone frowned at her sister. "He's just goin' to get him patched up and make him disappear for a little while."

"But won't someone suspect that something happened to Antonio? I'm sure that he's been missed by now." Mona couldn't help the nervousness that pervaded her mind.

"Yeah, well, there's nothing we can do about that. My primary concern is just makin' sure that no one knows where we are for now. We only need one more day." Simone walked toward the kitchen, following the scent of the food with Mona hot on her heels. "And then I'll have one of my friends return Lyle's car to him."

Toots, who was still in the kitchen, had seamlessly shifted into the role of hostess, reaching into the cabinets and drawers for plates, forks, and glasses. "We were waitin' on you to get here before eatin'," she informed Simone while pulling out the dishware. "I stopped off at Pappasitos Mexican Cantina on the way back. There's too much food for us to eat, but I wanted to be sure there was somethin' that everyone would like."

"Are you sure that you weren't followed here?" Mona ignored Toots and continued questioning Simone, who began opening the containers of food. Although Mona had awakened from her nap with a healthy appetite, it had entirely disappeared with the news of having nearly been found. "Is Sophie going to be safe here?"

"Relax. Nobody followed me. I took the scenic route back to make sure of that. The cabdriver made so much money off me, I'll bet he shut down for the day after droppin' me off a few blocks from here."

"Honey, your sister is smart, okay? In our line of work, we have dealt with every form of scum for a living and we both know how to shut them down."

"Ain't that the truth." Simone reached for a plate to start filling with food. "And if you had seen Toots with that gun, you'd be glad that she's on our side!"

"Stop it, girl, okay?" Toots reached for a plate as well. "He's just lucky to be livin', 'specially since he called you the p-word, okay? He ain't nobody that people would mind seein' dead."

Mona, who had yet to fully convert back to the tougher frame of mind she'd known as a teenager, felt baffled as she watched the two women converse so placidly. She believed that the part of herself willing to act in self-defense had already kicked in, but she doubted she'd ever possess the capacity to deliberately harm a subdued, unarmed individual. Knowing what Simone had experienced over the past ten years, Mona was doing her best to understand and accept this coldblooded side of her sister. And God only knew what Toots may have gone through in her own life. "How can you be so calm and so cold?"

Toots and Simone looked at each before Simone responded.

"Because we're both well acquainted with the rough side of the streets." Simone handed her plate to Mona. "Just like you were when we were kids." Mona mechanically accepted the plate that Simone offered, but stared at her sister without budging. "Toots is actually the heroine today, though. She was all over that guy."

"Weren't either of you scared?"

"Of course we were scared!" Toots practically shouted over her shoulder as she prepared her own plate of food.

"But we can't let that stop us from doin' what needs to be done, can we?" Simone reached for another plate and began putting food on it. "By the way, that plate I just gave you is for you. We haven't eaten since this mornin' and you need to eat somethin'."

Mona looked at the food: enchiladas, Spanish rice, refried beans, chicken fajitas. It was enough food for both her and Sophie to eat. But Mona's mind wasn't ready to shift gears yet. "So who do you think Antonio works for?"

"Right now, I think he's linked to the Escobars. He was just tailin' me, though, until the real killers could get there." Simone began walking to the dining area as she spoke.

"Why do you think that?" Mona followed Simone and set the plate heaping with food down on the table.

"Because he didn't have a gun on him."

Toots carried her own plate into the dining area. "Honey, what does your baby like to eat? I'm gonna fix her plate, okay?"

Unexpectedly distracted with the question, Mona had to pause to collect her thoughts before answering. "Uh, can you please just bring me another empty plate? I'm going to give her some of my food. I couldn't possibly eat all this." Mona gestured toward the plate that Simone had prepared and Toots's eyes followed. The amount of food was enough for a giant.

"I see your point." Toots went back into the kitchen for another plate.

"By the way," Simone said between bites, "we lifted Antonio's cell phone. It's in my purse. I think you should take a look at it, see if you recognize any of the phone numbers."

"Okay." Mona looked around, feeling lost. "Where's your purse?"

"In the living room." Simone took another big bite of a burrito. "It's the black Motorola phone."

Mona went into the living room, located Simone's purse, and soon dug out the phone that Simone described. After turning on the phone, Mona first tried the address book. Empty. Now she tried the incoming and outgoing call lists as she walked back into the dining area.

"See anything?" Simone was transferring some of Mona's food onto Sophie's plate as the young girl, who now sat between her aunt and Toots, watched with hungry eyes.

"Not yet." Mona continued scrolling, taking her time to thoughtfully consider each phone number on the incoming calls list. Suddenly, she caught her breath at seeing a number she had come to know all too well.

Simone immediately dropped her fork. "What's wrong?"

Mona's throat went dry and her hand began to tremble. Unable to speak, she walked to Simone and pointed out the phone number that had upset her.

"What?" Simone looked at the number and shook her head. "Is that somebody you know?"

Mona nodded jerkily.

"Well, who is it, honey?" Toots's mouth was full, but she discarded manners as her eyes bulged from her head.

After several unsteady breaths, Mona finally looked from Simone to Toots. "It's the last person I expected to see," she croaked.

"Who?" Toots and Simone nearly yelled in unison.

Mona swallowed hard. "It's Detective Harold Monroe."

—⁓—

"Damned cops!" Simone paced in the living room as Mona sat sullenly on a sofa and Toots stood near her fireplace with her arms crossed. So that the women could discuss the new information, Sophie had again been banished to Toots's bedroom with her food. It was obvious that Sophie had grown weary of the confinement since this time she started whining, but Mona had been unmoved and undeterred. After a short bout of pouting, Sophie had gone to the bedroom, but none of the women uttered a word until they heard the door click softly behind her. "I told you that we can't trust 'em! None of 'em!"

"B-but there has to be an explanation for this," Mona stuttered unhappily.

"That's right," Simone spun to face her. "And the explanation is that he's one of them, probably been takin' payoffs to look the other way so Aaron's buddies could traffic their drugs in and out of the city for years."

"It just doesn't make sense, though." Mona ran her hands through her hair before reaching for her purse. "Mind if I smoke in here, Toots?"

"No, honey, go right ahead. I'm used to smoke. As a matter of fact, I think I might have one myself, okay?"

She walked over to Mona and accepted a cigarette and lit it after Mona lit her own.

Mona immediately took a long drag and closed her eyes to concentrate on the disbursement of the nicotine as it traveled through her lungs, through her veins, and finally to her brain. She relaxed a little, again opening her eyes to watch her sister pace angrily around the room.

"It's all coming together now," Simone sneered. "Harold has been privy to our whereabouts every step of the way until we came here. He's the one who hand-picked the officers ordered to guard us at the hotel. He called you so you'd leave Jocelyn's house the other day when someone tried to blow you up."

"But you just said yourself that he didn't know we were coming here," Mona feebly attempted to reason. Something inside her was crumpling under the weight of an inexplicable grief she'd never experienced before this moment.

"Yeah, he didn't know where we went so he had one of his thug friends to stake out Galveston, maybe watch my house in case we showed up."

Toots heaved a cloud of smoke into the air. "Don't be so disappointed, honey," she cooed to Mona, who was clearly distraught about the detective. "Cops are human, imperfect like the rest of us, okay? They see a lot of crap in their jobs and some of 'em become exactly what they hate. It happens."

"You sound like you feel sorry for 'em, Toots." Simone's voice was thick with resentment.

Toots shrugged and puffed on the cigarette. "I guess I do. You forgot that the love of my life was a cop."

Simone rolled her eyes as Mona exhaled smog into the air, still feeling rattled, but also more clearheaded. "So what happened to him?"

"Far as I know, he's still out there, still a cop." She huffed and took another drag on her cigarette. "At least, he collects a paycheck from the city, but he's just as crooked as the men locked up in the pen. Wasn't always like that, though. Used to be nice, real good to me, okay? But the money on the streets was just too much temptation for him to keep turnin' down. He could make his annual pay in one night, okay?" Toots shook her head, the hurt riddling her face as she recalled the man. "So I had to let him go. Couldn't go nowhere with a man like that unless I wanted to live my life lookin' over my shoulder."

"But if he changed, you'd take him back, wouldn't you?" Mona's heart went out to Toots although she couldn't imagine how it must be to love a man – or a woman – that way.

"In a heartbeat, ya hear me? In a heartbeat."

Simone appeared to be simmering at the women's conversation. "I hope you're not implyin' that my sister should forgive Detective Monroe for tryin' to get her killed!"

"You know I'm not sayin' that." Toots looked at Mona. "I just wantcha to try seein' things the way he probably sees 'em. I get the feelin' that you thought you'd met somebody who you could trust, right?"

Mona nodded and looked down while sucking on her cigarette.

"Somewhere in history, he could've been the man you thought you met. You may never know what changed him, but now you have to accept that he's a stranger to you, okay? You don't really know him."

"He's not just a stranger," Simone nearly screamed. "He's our enemy!" She went to Mona and grabbed her sister's shoulders until her eyes snapped up to meet hers. "Your enemy. Understand?"

Mona's eyes again dropped to the floor. She nodded weakly and placed her cigarette to her mouth before Simone could see that her lips were trembling.

—⁓—

He had driven around most of the city of Houston with no luck at locating Mrs. Baker or her sister. But he was confident that they would eventually turn up – dead or alive in light of the number of people searching for them. Hopefully, Mrs. Baker would not be killed because his mission would then be terminated without the payoff he'd been promised. And it could also be a black mark on his record, on his spotless reputation for being reliable and effective. That would not be acceptable at all.

After losing Mrs. Baker at La Cocina earlier that day, he had initially taken post outside Mr. Baker's house to observe any unusual activity. There was none. Mr. Baker was definitely keeping a low profile these days now that the police had raided his home and his employers had told him to get lost. The shmuck hadn't seen it coming, he chuckled to himself. God, what a dope! But that's what power does to a person, makes them believe they're invincible when they're actually living in a house of cards. Once people start thinking they can't be touched, they start making mistakes, start trusting the wrong people, fail to destroy incriminating documents, say the wrong things in front of the wrong people, screw with things that don't belong to them.

But he wouldn't make that mistake. He considered himself privileged to learn from watching other people topple, from sometimes being the operative tasked to topple them. Each time he was called into action, he would force himself to assess a favorite question: Why did this person fail? And nearly as often: Why must this person meet his end at my hands? Inevitably, the answer was carelessness brought on by overconfidence. Mr. Baker was just another mule that had been too drunk with his perceived power to see that he had unwittingly stepped in his own manure. Even now, he had not figured it out, but the stinking smell had certainly driven everyone else away. Other than the cops parked a few houses away – and himself, of course – not a soul bothered to pay a visit to Mr. Baker. This stakeout was pointless.

He soundlessly stole his way back to his car, which was parked a few blocks over. No sooner had he started the engine when his cell phone began to vibrate. Only his current client had this phone number so he didn't bother to glance at the caller ID. He would dispose of this phone when his mission was completed.

"Yes, sir?"

"Where are you?" His client sounded agitated, but he ignored it.

"I'm leaving Mr. Baker's house."

"Why would you ever go there?" Now he sounded alarmed. "The police are still watching him."

"I know that. Don't worry. They didn't see me." He pulled away from the curb and began driving out of the River Oaks subdivision.

"I hope you're right about that because the last thing I need is for you to be caught sneaking around that house!"

He didn't respond. Anger solved nothing and he needed to remain clearheaded.

"Where are you going now? Any leads from your network of helpers?"

"No. Mrs. Baker has had her cell phone turned off since leaving the restaurant so we haven't been able to track her yet."

"And she hasn't been using her credit cards either. I've checked."

"Guess she's smarter than we thought." He smiled since he knew the comment stabbed at his client's sensibilities.

The man sighed. "I suppose you're right." Silence. "So what's your next move?"

"I'm going to drive to League City and check out her sister's apartment there. Maybe I'll find something that leads me to them."

"Or maybe they're at the apartment!" The man suddenly sounded excited.

"That's a negative. If they were there, I would have heard it on the police scanner. I've been monitoring their transmissions for hours now."

"Then maybe you shouldn't go there. The police may be watching the place."

"They don't have the manpower to watch it round the clock, especially since Mrs. Baker voluntarily lost the cops."

"Yes, I'm sure you're right about that."

He wanted to laugh at his client's desperation, but managed to contain himself. His voice still sounded emotionless. "I'm also considering driving to Galveston. I understand that the sister has a beach house there."

"I'd be surprised if you find them there, but it doesn't hurt to check in case they're laying low."

"Right."

"Just remember that I don't want Mrs. Baker killed or injured in any way. If anything happens to her, you will receive no additional payment for your services."

"Understood."

"I must say that I'm very displeased with your work today. One would think that keeping an eye on a woman with a babbling kid would be child's play. But perhaps we've discovered your Achilles heel. Perhaps your superiors should be advised that you should only be used for sniper assignments."

The man nearly choked on the explicators that instantly stampeded his brain. His face turned a fiery red but he remained silent. He had already known that his reputation was at stake, but hearing his career being threatened almost provoked him to track down his client and use him for target practice.

"I gather from your silence that you get my meaning."

"Loud and clear," he fumed.

"I'm glad we understand each other. You know how to reach me if you learn something useful. I'll call you if I hear anything." He disconnected.

For a few seconds, the man battled against crushing his cell phone in his palm. Anger solves nothing, he reminded himself. Anger solves nothing. Finally, he relaxed his grip on the phone and let it drop into the passenger seat. He then forced himself to focus on the issue at hand – locating Mrs. Baker. It would be nightfall by the time he reached League City. He would survey the area before venturing into Miss Edwards' apartment, but he was reasonably certain that no police were staking out the place. Still, checking out the scene before acting was plain prudent and justified. He wouldn't invest too much confidence in his expectations. He would wait and see when he got there.

Just thinking along such sensible lines of reason relieved the anger that had seized him a short time ago. He was highly skilled at mastering his emotions rather than allowing them to dictate his actions. In fact, being consistently logical enabled him to excel at his job. He knew he was more than good. He was great, even excellent. But he wasn't perfect. He would never tell himself that he was perfect because that would be opening the door for him to be toppled by overconfidence.

His heart rate was normal again and his mind free of emotional clutter. He was approaching highway 610 East, which would eventually take him to highway 45 South. From there, it would be around thirty minutes to League City and possibly to a lead on where Mrs. Baker was now hiding out.

TWELVE

The following morning, Mona awakened with a head-ache that had to be evolving into a migraine. The hour was still predawn, the condo utterly silent, and Sophie was snoring softly beside her in their guest bed. Knowing that the impending morning sunlight would aggravate the pains short-circuiting her brain, Mona decided to lie where she was, keeping her eyes tightly shut as her only means of protection.

Mona considered that the headache was a result of not getting enough sleep last night, but that seemed unlikely since she and Sophie had enjoyed fairly rest-ful naps yesterday afternoon. She hated to admit it to herself, but her mind was actually grappling with the fact that Harold had turned out to be a sleazeball, news that still boggled her senses. Just thinking about it now caused the pounding to worsen, but Mona was unable to derail the train of thought. In particular, her emotional reaction to the situation was deeply unsettling. A few days earlier, the news of Harold's true nature would have simply been a confirmation of presumed deception, but at some recent point in time, something inside of her had warmed up to him without her realizing it. When in the world had that happened? Then again, why shouldn't it have happened? Harold had given her every reason to believe that he had wanted to protect her and Sophie. Or had he merely been out to gain her trust so she'd be easier to manipulate as Simone accused? The questions plagued her – and so did her throbbing head.

But there was another question that now presented itself to Mona: Had she become attracted to Harold in the midst of so much hell around her? If so, it would explain her sharp degree of disappointment now that she knew the truth about him. She pondered the idea and searched herself, calling his face to mind as well as their conversations over the past few days. Mona already recognized that she had a pattern of being attracted to people who emanated some form of power and control in their lives. She also acknowledged to herself that Harold had certainly exhibited these characteristics. But he also fell exceedingly short of a critical factor: he was a peasant compared to everyone else who had gained her attention over the years. He was really a nothing in the overall economic scheme of things. Rightly or wrongly, money was indelibly linked to power in Mona's mind, which meant that she couldn't be attracted to Harold. Rather, she must have unwisely connected her survival to his efforts to protect her. Now that this subconscious association had been abruptly swept away, Mona felt naked, more vulnerable than ever to the lowlifes who wanted her dead. And her fear for Sophie's life and safety had swelled at a staggering rate. That's why she had the headache. And that was also why she had to get out of bed. Today was the day that would resolve all these inner torments.

Mona was anxious about the activities that lay ahead, but she consoled herself that it was only one day in her life. Undoubtedly, it would be a long day, but also one that would pass like all others eventually did. And starting tomorrow, Mona was prepared to never look back again, to erase Aaron, Antonio, the dead guy in the hotel room, the lovers she had cheated with, Harold – nearly everyone and everything that had entered her life in the past ten years – from her mind. All that would survive would be Sophie and Simone, the truest loves of her life.

—⁂—

Mona slowly ambled into the dim kitchen and found a bottle of Aleve, hurriedly swallowed two pills, and then sat at the dining room table with her forehead resting atop her forearms. She hoped that the painkillers would do their job quickly because the blows assailing her head were making it increasingly difficult for her to think. And she really needed to think, to get prepared for the day.

God only knew how much time passed before Mona felt the pain begin to subside. She had not even bothered to glance at the electric clock at her bedside before emerging from the bedroom because she feared even the soft red glow that illuminated the digits. Sensing that the headache was slightly duller, she tested her luck by lifting her head slightly.

"What's wrong with you?" Simone entered the dining room on her way to the kitchen, pausing to examine her sister with concern.

"Headache," she whispered. "Would you please speak a little lower? Your voice is killing me right now." Mona dropped her head back to her forearms, the pain having been aggravated by Simone's talking.

She now also whispered, "Sorry. Did you take something for that?"

"Yes. Shhhhh. Please."

"Okay." Simone tiptoed into the kitchen to get a pot of coffee started with as little noise as possible while Mona remained still. After several moments passed, Mona again felt the pain subside and decided to test her luck once more by lifting her head around one foot above the table. Made it. Now she focused on the color black while rubbing her temples. Little by little, she began to feel more human. Eventually, she heard Simone pull a chair out and sit beside her with her coffee.

"Feelin' better yet?"

"A little, but keep your voice low to speed it up."

"Okay." Simone tipped her cup to her lips and watched her sister. "Think you'll be good to go in a few hours?" She was whispering again.

"I'll be ready. I have to be." Mona continued rotating her fingers over her temples, keeping her eyes closed, and her mind focused on complete blackness.

She and Simone sat in silence for several more minutes before Simone finally spoke again. "It's almost seven-thirty. We need to leave by eleven o'clock if you're serious about the shooting lessons."

Mona didn't bother to respond.

"You do still want 'em, right?" Simone pressed.

"Of course." Mona tried opening her eyes to slits, testing her reaction to light. It wasn't as bad as she had expected so she opened them wider to look at her sister while still rubbing her temples.

"I know you're not happy about the plan, but it's the only way to get everybody off your back."

"I know."

"If you start to have second thoughts, just think about Sophie growin' up without her mother. Think about how she would feel about that."

Mona was silent. Again testing the migraine's diminishing rate, she slowly stopped rubbing her temples. Thankfully, she confirmed that another giant step had been made toward recovery. Now she stared at her sister, astonished at her calm demeanor. "You're not at all afraid or stressed, are you?"

Simone set down her coffee and leaned toward Mona. "How many times do we have to go over that? How many times do I have to tell you that we can't let fear get in our way?" She paused as she looked into Mona's eyes. "Do you wanna stay here while I'm gone? Because the truth is that I really don't need you around anyway."

"I'm going!" Mona's voice rose before she thought about the consequences. Instantly, her head began to throb again and she was forced to rub her temples. "I'd be worried sick if you went by yourself."

"Are you sure?"

"Yes, dammit, I'm sure!" She now closed her eyes again to help reduce the pain. "You're right, I don't like it, but I don't see any other way. As much as I've tried, I just don't see it." Mona sighed unhappily.

Simone straightened up again and Mona heard the coffee mug briefly scrape the table as Simone picked it up. "Okay, but you're welcome to change your mind at any time."

Mona chose to remain silent, forced to again rest her forearms on the table and lower her head to rest atop them. It was all she could do not to groan, but she adamantly resisted the urge to prevent Simone from insisting that she would be better off left behind.

—ɯ—

A few hours later, Mona was showered and dressed in jeans, a brown Gap t-shirt, and the tennis shoes she'd purchased. Although her eyes were still puffy, the headache had diminished to a minor pain she would simply have to cope with. She felt like she could function again, which was a huge relief since Simone had hurled out several warnings about leaving without her if she needed a caregiver.

Mona decided to check her cell phone voice mail messages, taking care to do so from Toots's landline. Apparently, Simone had seen a movie several years ago that revealed how technology could be used to pinpoint the origins of cell phone signals, which translated into the users being located. If the cops were desperate enough, Simone had reasoned, then it was best to assume that they would employ this technology to find Mona. As a result, Simone had been firm that Mona must turn off and remove the battery from her cell phone when they left Houston yesterday. If she had a problem with this deprivation, she would need to buy a pay-as-you-go cell phone and register it under a different name, if at all, as Simone had done upon divorcing her abusive husband.

While Sophie, who was still in her pajamas, ate a bowl of cereal, Mona reached for the kitchen phone and dialed the phone number for her voice mail service. She had five new messages, none of which she really wanted to hear, but she had to know if Richard had attempted to reach her with an update.

The first message was from Harold, of course, since he had called yesterday as she'd been speeding away from La Cocina. He sounded genuinely angry on the pretense of being concerned about her safety. Or was he pretending? Maybe he wasn't faking the anger, but the reason he gave for his concern was the lie. She rapidly deleted the message.

The second message was from Lyle congratulating her on making a clean getaway from his restaurant. He assured her that the policemen were still scouring the nearby area since no one fitting Mona's, Sophie's, or Simone's descriptions had been seen leaving. He had left the message around fifteen minutes after they had snuck out. Just when Mona began to feel somewhat warm with gratitude to Lyle, he closed out the message with a question of whether he'd get some "pearl jam" for his benevolence. "Uh!" She deleted that message as well.

The next two messages were from Harold, who had regained control of himself before calling her again. He apologized for coming off like a jerk in the first message. He also urged her to call him as soon as possible, to please let him know that she was safe. If she were willing to consider a different protection arrangement with the police, he also had some options to discuss. Harold certainly did sound sincere. Mona listened to both messages twice, concentrating on his tone of voice. The man should have been an actor because his degree of sincerity had to be difficult to fake. She finally deleted the messages.

The last message was from Richard, who was also asking her to call in and confirm her safety. The police were hassling him, particularly Detective Monroe, and Richard was feeling pressured to get a response to them. Mona briefly toyed with the idea of returning his call, but decided to stay with her first instinct and remain remote. She had never fully trusted Richard since he had worked for Aaron and there was no reason she should treat him any differently than the police right now. The important thing was that she had confirmed through the messages that no one knew where she was.

She hung up the phone and wordlessly looked at Sophie, who continued to eat her cereal, but was obviously getting full. If all went well today, they would be starting a new life tomorrow. They would all be free again. Thank God.

"Do you want some orange juice, munchkin?" Mona walked over to Sophie and rubbed the top of the girl's uncombed head.

She just shook her head while chewing the cereal already in her mouth.

Mona squatted down and kissed Sophie's cheek. "You're going to have so much fun with Miss Toots today! She's at the store right now renting movies for you and then she's going to Shipley's Donuts to buy some of those chocolate-covered doughnuts that you love."

"Is she going to get *The Lion King*?" Sophie's eyes grew wide with the question.

Mona laughed. "Of course! I told her that if she didn't get anything else, she must get *The Lion King*."

"Yea!"

"Can you make any more noise?" Simone smiled as she entered the room with her duffle bag and set it down on her way into the kitchen.

Sophie let out another, "Yea!" louder than ever and giggled.

"The girl has got the lungs of an elephant!" Simone called from the kitchen.

"Tell me about it." Mona rubbed Sophie's head again and stood up. "Now I want you to mind Miss Toots while I'm gone like we agreed, okay?"

"Yes, Mommy."

"And don't forget that I'll be back tomorrow morning, maybe before you wake up."

"Okay." Sophie looked up at Mona and smiled as Simone exited the kitchen with a banana.

Mona glanced at her sister's makeshift meal. "Is that all you're gonna have?"

"It's all I need." She took a bite. "What have you eaten this morning?"

Mona scowled and rolled her eyes. She had not eaten anything, which Simone already knew.

"I'm back!" Toots called from the living room as she closed the door behind her. "Got some good stuff, too!"

Without preamble, Sophie promptly scrambled into the living room to make a grab for the movies. Meanwhile, Simone retrieved her duffle bag and followed Mona into the living room. For a few moments, the room was filled with Sophie's excited screeches upon pulling out *The Lion King* DVD.

Toots laughed as she set down the doughnuts. "I guess I know what we're watchin' first, okay?"

Mona used a few more minutes to look at her daughter, committing the moment to her memory and feeling fearful that she might never see her child again. Ultimately, Mona was caught in a catch-22: if she didn't follow Simone's plan today, Sophie might very well be orphaned at some point in the unforeseeable future. If Mona did follow the plan, something might go terribly wrong and Sophie would nevertheless be deprived of her mother. At this point, she could rely on only one fact – she was possibly damned either way. Mona fought off the tears that involuntarily sprang to her eyes.

"We'd better go." Simone reached for Mona's arm and gently tugged her toward the door.

"One second." Mona turned back to Sophie. "Come give Mommy a hug, sweetie." She threw her arms open and Sophie ran into them, still clinging to *The Lion King* DVD. "I love you very, very much."

"I love you, too, Mommy." Sophie looked up at Mona and smiled. It was heartbreakingly innocent.

"Let's go." Simone was reaching for the doorknob.

"Okay." Mona swiped at her nose and then reached into her purse for a tissue as Sophie rushed to the DVD player to get the movie started.

"Don't worry about her," Toots touched Mona's arm. "She'll be fine."

"I don't doubt that, Toots." Mona smiled at Toots's reassurance. "Thanks for keeping her for me."

"It's no problem, honey. Now you two go handle your business."

Mona wordlessly nodded and turned back to Simone, who was silently waiting at the door. Finally, the two sisters exited the condo and took the elevator down to the garage, which was located beneath the building. Toots, who owned two cars, was allowing them to use her black Nissan Xterra, a common vehicle that should enable them to blend in easily.

As they pulled out of the garage, Simone hesitated and looked at her sister, who had grown pale and deathly silent. "Are you sure you wanna go?"

Mona pursed her lips and stared straight ahead. "Just drive."

—⁂—

He was on his last guess at where Mrs. Baker could possibly be – Galveston. After carefully combing through the meager belongings that Miss Edwards had inside her tiny League City apartment, he'd been briefly irked to find nothing that led him anywhere.

Now, as he approached the Galveston city line, he began to put more thought into what he knew about

Miss Edwards. According to the dossier provided to him, she had lived on the streets for a while after running away from her mother's home as a teenager. While working as a stripper, she had earned her GED and later graduated from college after several years of part-time classwork. The police had reason to believe that Miss Edwards had murdered her uncle, a known pedophile who they'd been unable to lock up for various technical reasons. What did all that say about Miss Edwards? For one thing, she was obviously smart. She also had the potential to be dangerous when she was provoked. He wondered how good she was with a gun these days. Probably better than one would expect since her dossier included a record of shooting lessons she had taken several years ago. The woman was obviously serious about protecting herself if she ever had man problems again.

Given Miss Edwards' known history, what could he expect a woman like her to do since she was highly motivated to protect her sister, as already proven by the shooting at the hotel a few days earlier? Her first concern would be preserving Mrs. Baker's life, of course. Her second concern would be preserving her renewed relationship with Mrs. Baker. To accomplish both objectives, she may be planning to run again just as she had fled her mother's home as a teenager. That was usually the option that people took when they felt threatened. And it would have been a predictable option if Miss Edwards had not troubled herself with those shooting lessons. This information implied that she was inclined to punish anyone else who tried to push her around. And if she had actually been responsible for her uncle's death as suspected, then she'd also demonstrated a vengeful quality that surpassed that of most women.

He tapped the steering wheel as he mulled over all these facts. If Miss Edwards was the type to punish anyone who attacked her, wasn't she just as likely to punish anyone who attacked her sister? And, if so, who was she likely to punish for Mrs. Baker's current peril? It didn't take long for the answer to leap into his mind. He immediately stomped on the brakes, nearly causing his car to be rear-ended and then sideswiped by oncoming traffic as he swerved to a freeway exit already on his right. Barely missing the concrete slabs that marked the end of the exit, he skidded onto the feeder and sped to the nearest U-turn. There was no doubt in his mind that his trip to Galveston had been an enormous mistake, one that may have cost him valuable time.

THIRTEEN

It was after midnight when Simone pushed her way into the nightclub, a crowded hotspot filled with twenty-somethings wearing naval rings, blouses with deep V-cuts, micro skirts, and "fuck me" pumps. Women were gyrating around the dance floor, tossing their hair to the beat of the rhythmic music, parading themselves and flirting with the ogling men who either sat at the bar or animatedly thrust their own pelvises back at the women on the dance floor. The scene was exactly the sort that Simone had come to despise while working as a stripper. She absolutely detested the fact that warped social conditioning bred the lie that a woman's sexuality was her most auspicious asset, compelling women to put themselves on display as though conjuring images of sex was their only option for arresting the male imagination. She had learned in college that this subliminal way of thinking had been perpetuated via the media, which then fed the current American culture. It was a terrible degradation that Simone hoped to see ended in her lifetime.

Simone's unspoken criticism was hypocritical in light of her working history, which had vigorously spurred her desire to someday embark on a profession that appreciated her mind and her character. Stripping had always been a temporary method to pay her bills and her tuition as Simone could not envision being a permanent, willing participant in a lifestyle that transformed her sexuality into a burden. Many of her stripper friends felt that they were empowered by their bodies, boasting of limitless numbers of sugar daddies, but Simone longed to be empowered by her intellect. When a stripper, she'd never gotten comfortable with having men's eyes raping her body as she danced on stage and out of reach. For the perverts who tried to let their hands follow their eyes when she walked to her car after shows, her best friend – Mr. Smith and Wesson – rapidly restored their manners.

Simone subconsciously patted her purse now, feeling the hard gun beneath the fabric as she glanced around in search of her prey. To ensure she would blend in with the crowd as well as attract the intended attention, she was wearing a skimpy white blouse that barely hung onto her body by the tiniest spaghetti straps. Her miniskirt fell just below her butt, rendering the options of sitting down or bending over plain obscene. Simone had pulled it all together with a wig of neck-length black hair that was combed in gentle wisps around her face and just enough makeup to sweeten her features. In short, she looked like a really nice slut. And, following Mona's advice, she reeked of a particular Elizabeth Taylor perfume called Diamonds.

After pressing her way through the congested dance floor, Simone found a space to stand at the bar, where she could easily scan the club. She already knew he was here because his car was parked outside. The bartender took her order just as a wannabe playboy tried to pick her up only to be summarily blown off with an indifferent wave of her hand. He had continued to stand beside her, his lip curled with indignant anger, until she'd opened her purse and shown him the gun. Poof! He was gone like a puff of smoke.

Simone casually continued to screen the crowd as she sipped her nonalcoholic piña colada. When her eyes drifted to a corner furthest from the dance floor, she finally spotted him. He was sitting in a booth with a woman at his right rubbing her hand beneath his shirt. Sitting to his left was another woman, who appeared to have her tongue in his ear. It was a nasty human sandwich that made Simone's skin crawl. She watched without moving just yet, choosing to observe his reaction to the women. There would be no sense in commencing with the plan tonight if his attention was already consumed with his current set of admirers. She needed to be mysterious when she caught his eye, enticing, but not familiar. That objective would be ruined if she got too close at the wrong time.

Simone continued to wait and to watch, rejecting more wannabes who she couldn't hear talking over the music anyway. Around twenty minutes later, she saw what she was looking for on her quarry's face: boredom. The women clinging to him in the booth were simply not challenging enough to hold his interest. She had been coached about that quality in him and was prepared to strike just the right balance between independence and embarrassingly horny tonight. Sweetness and reluctant wantonness, a fairly typical combination that appealed to most men of his caliber.

She should have been nervous, but this environment was one she knew all too well. Simone coolly slid away from the bar and began easing toward his booth. She then found a black metal pole nearby to lean against as though she were merely in search of a dance partner. More men offered themselves while she posed against the pole, but she ignored them all while allowing her gaze to intermittently fall on his slack face. He would have been handsome, she thought, but there was something contemptible about him that spoiled his regal features. Simone could spot it a mile away. Finally, he saw her and she quickly dropped her eyes to the floor as though flustered to have been caught looking. She then deliberately refused to look in his direction again, expecting that her failure to do so would eventually prompt him to act if he found her attractive. And since Mona had adeptly selected her clothes, makeup, and wig for the evening, Simone was certain that he was attracted. Before long, he walked into the trap.

"A beautiful woman like you shouldn't be here all by yourself." The voice was husky in her ear and she could smell the bourbon on his breath. "What's your name?"

She pretended shyness as she turned to face Aaron and smiled innocently at him. "My name is Dawn."

—∽∾—

He had yet to locate Mrs. Baker, but he was betting that he'd find her by sticking close to her husband. He had to be extremely careful, however, because the police were also tagging along, dogging every one of Mr. Baker's footsteps. They didn't even bother to covertly trail the man. As he'd backed out of his driveway earlier that evening, they had immediately turned on their headlights and pulled forward, soon afterward following him with little more than perhaps ten feet between their Mercury Sable and his convertible BMW. It would have been laughable if he weren't in such dire need to locate Mrs. Baker before somebody put a hole in her head.

Once the officers were on their way, he had fired up his own engine and begun to tail them, trusting that he wouldn't lose Mr. Baker since the police obviously were not going to. But he already knew where Mr. Baker was going. Having essentially led the life of a nymphomaniac for most of his adult years, Mr. Baker had an established pattern of club hopping, frequenting whatever spots were newest, upscale, and filled with ripe women. His choice of late, according to the dossier resting beneath his car seat, was a place called En Boga, which was Spanish for "in vogue." All the young rich girls around Houston went there to score a little dope and often times a one-night stand. Saturday nights were always the busiest, but Sunday nights still boasted a healthy number of vivacious clientele that Mr. Baker picked off like peaches. Apparently, his sex drive had not suffered despite the ongoing crisis that threatened his uninterrupted freedom. Or perhaps he thought he had something to celebrate tonight since his wife had disappeared. Mr. Baker probably thought that no news of her whereabouts was good news given the various attempts to put her six feet underground in the past week.

Mr. Baker, the police, and their secret escort all cruised into the En Boga parking lot, at which point Mr. Baker left his car with the valet while the police continued driving around in search of a parking space. They seemed to be in no hurry, which implied that someone was already planted inside to keep Mr. Baker in sight. While the police went one direction, the operative went another, already knowing that his blue jeans were not acceptable attire for the establishment. Frankly, he didn't want to go in because the crowd would suffocate him. He'd never liked being around large groups of people so he was grateful that the police were monitoring Mr. Baker so closely. And if Mrs. Baker happened to show up, which he doubted would be the case in such a public domain, he would see her from where he now parked within view of the club's entrance. He could also see the front fender of the policemen's car. He didn't need to see their faces and he certainly didn't want to be in their line of view.

Once positioned in a nearly empty parking lot across the street from the club, he reached for his brownbag dinner – a tasteless rice cake with some sugarless peanut butter to add a little flair.

—⚒—

A masterful palette of colors blinded Simone as Aaron leaned in to kiss her neck in the booth they now shared by themselves. Earlier in the evening, the club lights had been so dim that the occupants could hardly see in front of themselves, a condition that coaxed the more primal forces in the patrons who were intoxicated or lonely or both. Now at 2:00 AM sharp, someone had thrown the lights and Simone was momentarily blinded as she pretended to be somewhat receptive to Aaron's lips. He had no idea that he was kissing an enemy, a woman he'd only glimpsed in photos whenever he carelessly crossed his wife's bedroom. Simone had looked much different in those photos, though. She'd either been a small child or an introverted teenager who shied from the camera. Back then she had smiled more often, had more hope in her eyes and greater expectations of the world. Much had changed since then. Not only had her body matured into that of a woman, but the light in her eyes had long ago been extinguished by the very world she had once been eager to explore. Now she beheld the world through experienced eyes that hardly cloaked traces of both her past pains and the reserves of potential viciousness that lay just beneath the surface. If Aaron had bothered to look into Simone's eyes at that very moment, he may have left her at the club and unwittingly saved himself.

"This place is closing down for the night," he panted in her ear. "Why don't you come back to my house with me, baby. I can tell you need it tonight just as bad as I do." He went for her lips, but she coyly turned her head away.

"I don't know, Aaron. I have to get up for work at six o'clock in the morning."

"So call in, baby." He placed a hand on her waist and squeezed it. "Tell 'em you're feeling sick or something."

Actually, she did feel sick. The more she endured his hands and his lips, the more her stomach churned with revulsion. "Maybe you're right."

"Of course I'm right." He licked his lips as he glanced down at her panties, which were now exposed as she'd known they would be when she sat down.

He took her hand and began tugging her out of the booth. "Come on. Let's get outta here."

"Oh, okay." She smiled uncertainly while allowing him to clutch her hand. Together they filed out of the club with the rest of the patrons and began walking toward the valet stand.

"Where's your car?"

"In the shop. I took a cab." She subconsciously touched the fabric on her purse for reassurance as she'd done countless times throughout the night.

Aaron handed the valet ticket to the next available attendant so his BMW would be retrieved. While they waited, he again wrapped a hand around her waist and pulled her against him. "I can't wait to see you naked. You've got one of the hottest bodies I've ever seen."

Inwardly, Simone grimaced. Outwardly, she cast her eyes downward and whispered a polite, "Thank you."

"You're welcome, baby." His voice had grown hoarse and Simone was relieved when his car arrived. Aaron opened the passenger door for her as the attendant ran around the front of the car for his tip.

As Simone sat in the BMW, the beginnings of nervousness beset her. She cradled her purse over her crotch to cover her panties as Aaron took his seat on the driver's side and punched his foot down on the accelerator.

—✕—

Mona had waited for the police to follow Aaron from the house before emerging from a row of bushes down the street. She had then raced as quickly as she could to Aaron's house and ran to the back, where she had entered the garage in search of a small stepping box to place against the fence in case she needed the getaway option later.

Now Mona crouched with silent impatience behind some rose bushes near one of the kitchen windows. Her view inside the house was reasonably unobstructed from this vantage point because the floor plan included a long hallway from the kitchen to the living room. She couldn't see the couches or armchairs where Aaron and Simone might sit upon their arrival, but her line of sight was sufficient for her to see whether Simone hit any unplanned glitches.

Mona's legs were painfully numb due to her perpetual immobilization. She looked at her watch. It was after 2:00 AM, which meant that the club must be shutting down for the night by now. Had Simone been unsuccessful in her ploy to seduce Aaron, she would have called Mona's new disposable cell phone with the news a long time ago. So she remained where she was and continued to wait with a growing sense of foreboding. To relieve her nervous energy, she thought about Sophie and their life together after today. She also puffed on a cigarette, something she knew was a bad idea, but it was necessary under the circumstances.

Around twenty more minutes passed before Mona glimpsed Aaron's headlights beaming up the driveway. She promptly stamped out the cigarette and reached into her purse for the unregistered pistol that she had purchased earlier that day from yet another of Simone's thug contacts in Galveston. Simone had given her a quick shooting lesson that afternoon, but Mona didn't think she'd ever get comfortable with a gun. It just didn't feel right in her hands. As she awkwardly fumbled with holding the gun with her thumb near the safety, she clumsily dropped it and then spent frantic seconds pawing the grass around her until she felt the gun beneath her hand. This brief episode did nothing to fuel her confidence! She worried that she couldn't operate the gun fast enough if called upon to rescue Simone. She also worried that she wouldn't be able to fire a shot at Aaron if it came down to it. Mona had not shared her misgivings with Simone, but Simone had probably figured it out since Mona consistently resembled a deer caught in the headlights whenever they discussed tonight's plan. At least, that was how Mona felt. And that was why Mona was in the bushes right now instead of in the house waiting to help her sister execute the most critical part of the plan.

She took a deep breath and exhaled slowly, stooping lower to ensure that Aaron wouldn't see her before entering the house with Simone. She clutched the gun the way Simone had shown her and held still, taking extra care that the cops tailing Aaron back to the house would not detect her.

—◊◊◊—

He watched Mr. Baker drive toward his residence accompanied by his trusting tot, but he had already stopped trailing the man by way of his police babysitters. So that he could continue to watch for Mrs. Baker's appearance, he got out of his car, hunched down, and trotted to the house, hiding behind various trees, bushes, and fences along the way. He considered sneaking past the police, but immediately rejected the idea because there was no real need for him to get closer to the house. Mr. Baker was not important to him. He decided to watch the house from the same post he had occupied the previous day. If his guess about Miss Edwards was correct, sooner or later he was sure that his true object of interest would show up.

—◊◊◊—

"I love your house!" Simone pretended childlike awe as she and Aaron entered through the kitchen. "I can't believe you're not married. Most women would die to live in a house like this." They progressed through a hall that led to the living room, each step marked by Simone's exaggerated enthusiasm about the home's furnishings and size.

"I'm glad you like it," Aaron drooled gruffly, failing to clarify his marital status as they reached the living room, which was already well lit by several lamps around the area. "Have a seat." He gestured toward one of the sofas nearest a stairwell and smoothly descended onto it. When Simone didn't comply, he patted a space beside him expectantly. "Come on, baby. You're not scared, are you?"

"No, I'm just a little thirsty. Would you mind getting me a drink?"

He paused, the annoyance flickering across his face before disappearing behind his icy smile. "Sure." Aaron grudgingly rose to his feet again. Rather than ask what she'd like to drink, however, he moved in to kiss her.

Simone expertly dodged his mouth for the millionth time that evening. "How 'bout that drink."

Vexed, Aaron clasped his hands together, struggling to maintain the appearance of being a gentleman. "Fine. What's your poison?" He began walking toward the bar, which was constructed directly beneath the stairwell behind the sofa. "We've got vodka –"

"We?"

"What?" He walked behind the bar and opened a cabinet containing multiple liquor bottles.

"You said we. I thought you weren't married." Simone opened her purse and began to reach in for the unregistered gun she had purchased for tonight's use.

Once again failing to respond to the question of his marital status, Aaron removed a bottle of vodka and opened another cabinet in search of glasses. "I'll have to get glasses from the kitchen." He walked away from the bar and crossed the room with the vodka bottle. Simone immediately froze with her hand still inside her purse.

"Vodka is fine with you, right?" He was already trudging toward the kitchen as he spoke.

Simone was breathless with anxiety. "Y-yes. Thank you." She watched Aaron walk down the hallway that led to the kitchen and withdrew her hand from the purse with the gun in her clutch. She then lifted the gun up such that her right arm was straight and level with her line of sight in a firing position. After kicking off her high heels, she began her own quiet walk down the hallway, cautiously listening for the sounds of Aaron preparing her drink. She deliberately halted when there was an inexplicable silence in the kitchen, resuming her trek only when she could hear the vodka being poured into the glass. Overwrought with nerves and apprehension, Simone didn't notice the ominous silhouette that she cast upon one of the living room windows she passed on her way to join Aaron.

—m—

If he saw it, he knew the police probably had. Hell, a blind man would have seen the shadow that just appeared through the curtains! He hadn't been able to make out whether the image was a woman's or a man's, but the gun had been unmistakable and his first suspicion was that Mrs. Baker may have been in the house when Mr. Baker got home. If so, she had more balls than he had given her credit for. If not, then maybe Mr. Baker had already hit a rough patch with the whore he'd brought home tonight.

He remained frozen in place, impatiently waiting for the police staking out the house to react. Sure enough, they were soon running across the yard with their guns drawn. He assumed that backup officers were also on the way.

—∽—

Mona could see Aaron standing in the kitchen through a window over the sink and her breath caught in her throat. She kept the pistol handle wrapped tightly in both hands, reasonably certain that she wouldn't need to use the weapon. Then the perfect night silence was abruptly disrupted by the sound of someone running toward Mona's hiding nook. Alarmed, she instinctively squatted lower behind the rose bushes while simultaneously looking around the driveway and the yard to identify the origin of the noise.

—∽—

Oblivious to everything except his salacious thoughts of Simone as he poured the vodka into two glasses, Aaron was momentarily confused when he heard a loud click behind him in the kitchen. He reflexively stopped filling the second glass and slowly turned around to see Simone pointing her gun at him. The click had been the safety being released.

"What in the hell are you doing?" His voice revealed his stark amazement at seeing the gun.

"What does it look like?" Simone warily edged a little closer, but remained safely out of arm's reach.

Aaron dazedly stared at her before anger took hold of him. "Who sent you, bitch? Tell me, was it Jesus, Carlos, who?"

"None of the above, asshole. Put your hands up where I can see 'em."

Aaron complied with a snarl on his face. "Who sent you?" he asked again between gritted teeth, never taking his eyes off the gun.

Simone fought to stifle the nervousness in her voice. "Your wife."

"My wife?" The stunned question hung in the air as Aaron scrutinized Simone with his feral eyes. Soon, he shook his head with a furious calm. "So you're Simone, right?" She didn't respond. "Right," he answered for her. "The coward couldn't face me herself so she sent her murdering sister." He again gazed intently at the gun still pointed at his head. "So would you be so kind as to tell me why the little woman wants me dead? I mean," he snorted, "she's already taken most of my money. What does killing me solve?"

"Don't play dumb, Aaron. We know you put a contract on her life when the cops made a deal with her. When word gets out that you're dead, no one will care about Mona anymore."

"I see." He looked toward the window over the sink. "But your plan has one critical flaw." He restored his scrutiny to Simone, using his eyes to molest her body as so many men had done in the strip clubs where she had danced.

"Die!" Simone fired at Aaron's head as he pitched himself sideways, dodging the bullet, which slammed into the wall. Before Simone could aim and fire again, the kitchen door exploded open.

"Freeze! Police!"

—⚏—

It was already too late when Mona realized that the police were responsible for the footsteps she heard racing up the driveway. As one of the officers ran past the rose bushes and headed for the kitchen back door, Mona knew that she had a decision to make. She glanced up and saw a clear view of Simone standing in the kitchen with her gun pointed at Aaron. In a few seconds, the cops would be on her and she might unthinkingly provoke a shootout that took her down. The mere thought was enough to provoke Mona to act despite the obvious risks to her own life.

She lurched from the bushes and ran to the kitchen door just as the cop kicked it in and yelled, "Freeze! Police!"

"You freeze, you son-of-a-bitch!" she screamed as loudly as she'd ever screamed in her life. She ran in and pointed her gun at the officer's back. The man immediately halted all movement as instructed and raised his hands upward to shoulder height as his partner tore into the kitchen from the hallway, having broken into the house through the front door. Both officers were now immobile, one staring at Simone with his hands raised as the other watched Mona with his gun pointed at her.

"Drop the gun, ma'am. Nobody has to get hurt here."

"No! You drop your gun or I'll shoot your partner." Mona's hand shook, but no one except her could see it.

Before another word was exchanged, Aaron lunged toward Simone, who was staring at her sister with shock. He swiftly grabbed Simone's gun and then threw his arm around her neck, pulling her against him such that her back was lodged against his chest. She began to choke against his locked forearm and reflexively gripped it in an attempt to relieve the pressure against her throat.

"Let her go!" Mona now swung her gun on Aaron, who had already trained his gun on her. They locked eyes for a millisecond as an evil smirk formed on Aaron's face. Not trusting her crude gun skills enough to fire at Aaron without harming Simone, Mona sensed the fragile fiber of bravery that she had so fiercely been reaching out for simply evaporating, leaving her broken inside at the worst possible moment. Her vision began to blur with tears when she saw Aaron's finger move on the trigger.

Mona closed her eyes, waiting to feel a bullet rip through her body and end her life, but she instead heard glass shatter somewhere in the kitchen followed by a weird thud. Without moving any of her limbs, she eased her eyes back open and saw that the kitchen window above the sink was broken. Aaron was nowhere to be seen.

"Drop the gun, ma'am!" The same officer commanded loudly from the hallway, his gun still trained on Mona.

Confused, her eyes darted around the kitchen, finding Simone, who was now staring at the kitchen floor with sheer alarm stamped on her face.

Mona finally looked downward, following Simone's eyes. To her absolute shock, Aaron lay there lifeless, his mouth and eyes wide with surprise as bright red blood oozed from somewhere in the back of his head.

She mutely lowered her gun to the floor then fell to her knees, grateful that she was still breathing and relieved that Simone was also still alive. Seconds later, she felt her sister's arms around her and they held onto each other as though their lives depended on it.

"Ma'am," the cop nearest to them spoke as the other kneeled beside Aaron's body and checked for a pulse. "You're both under arrest for conspiracy to commit murder and you," he pointed at Mona with his gun, "for also attempting to assault an officer."

"Start securing the crime scene, officer," a new voice cut off the policeman. "I'll take care of these two."

Mona didn't need to look up to identify the person who had joined them in the kitchen. Both she and Simone turned their heads at the same time to see Detective Harold Monroe towering over them.

FOURTEEN

As soon as she saw Detective Monroe, Simone glanced back down to the pistol that Mona had set on the floor. It was just within her reach.

"I wouldn't do that if I were you," Harold warned, having adeptly followed the direction of her gaze. "You're already in enough trouble as it is." He remained perfectly still until Simone's eyes again met his. He then stepped around the sisters, removed a handkerchief from his pocket, and picked up the gun as his eyes flickered over Aaron's body. "Is this the weapon used to kill Mr. Baker?" Harold first looked from Simone to Mona before raising his quizzical glance to the other two officers in the room.

"Sir," the policeman who had earlier been threatened with Mona's gun at his back spoke up, "the shots that killed Mr. Baker came through this window over the sink. I believe that the shooter fired two shots, both of which hit the victim in the back of his head. When we entered the house a short time ago, this lady here," he pointed at Simone, "was holding Mr. Baker at gunpoint so we attempted to –"

Harold held up his hand. "I get the picture. I'll read your report if I need to fill in any blanks. Our shooter is probably long gone, but one of you needs to check. And be careful not to destroy any evidence out there."

"Yes, sir." The officer who had been kneeling beside Aaron's body went to the kitchen door and paused. "The CSU is almost here. I can hear the sirens."

"Good." Harold's critical gaze returned to Mona and Simone, who were still holding each other on the floor. "Stand up," he ordered before grumbling, "I really hate to do this." He reached behind his back while keeping his eyes on the women, who were paralyzed with apprehension. "Stand up now!"

Both Mona and Simone trembled as they looked from Harold to the other officer, who stiffly holstered his gun without taking his eyes off the sisters. Slowly, they began to inch upward, rising together little by little, both of them troubled by the hand that had disappeared behind Harold's back.

"He's corrupt!" Simone suddenly shrieked at the officer. "He's goin' to kill us!"

"What?" Harold's hand rapidly reappeared with a set of handcuffs, which he innocently held up for everyone to see. "I'm just going to handcuff you!" He shook his head with offended disbelief and then spoke to the other officer. "Mind giving me a hand? I've only got one set of these with me."

The officer reached for the handcuffs attached to his belt and stepped closer to cuff Simone as the CSU vehicle loudly pulled into the driveway, the sirens still going at full blast. As Harold cuffed Mona, several police officers rushed into the house through the kitchen and living room, quickly surveying the scene.

"Jesus, I hate this crap," one of them groaned upon glimpsing Aaron's body on the kitchen floor. "I've gotta get a different job."

Finally feeling safe albeit fearful of what lie in store for them, Mona and Simone allowed Harold to lead them outside, whereupon they both observed a flurry of activity as officers searched the yard and hurried into the house with evidence kits.

"Have you heard yet, sir?" one of the young officers rushed up to Harold.

Harold squeezed Mona's and Simone's arms to halt their steps. "Heard what?"

"Well, sir, it looks like we've got a grassy knoll situation here. The round of fire that killed Mr. Baker came from somewhere by that fence behind those rose bushes. The thing is, nobody saw the shooter and nobody knows who it could've been."

—⁂—

Now that he finally knew where Mrs. Baker was, he had to keep an eye on her, an extremely risky business with so many policemen surrounding the house. With all the noise created by the police sirens, neighbors on the block had begun exiting their homes and standing on nearby sidewalks in their bathrobes to observe the ruckus. A few teenagers had even brought their cell phones with them to record the scene and the crowd, making it untenable for him to try blending in. The last thing he needed was his face plastered on TV because none of the River Oaks residents recognized him from some kid's amateur video. Every criminal psychologist and profiler would then want him found since common theories supported notions that shooters often returned to crime scenes to watch as the police investigated their handiwork.

He decided that his best option was to get far away and assume that Mrs. Baker would be brought in for questioning at the police station. After all, she had held a police officer at gunpoint and lived to tell about it. The woman had definitely proven to be full of more surprises than he would have ever expected given her posh lifestyle. He had been amazed upon taking cover behind a neighboring fence and then seeing Mrs. Baker run up the driveway. When he'd then seen her step into the kitchen with a gun drawn, he'd nearly dropped his own! Full of surprises indeed.

He had continued his diligent watch, moving in a little closer, but still sticking close to the fence, almost expecting to see the most stunning event possible: Mrs. Baker actually killing her husband or an officer. She had briefly seemed to be gaining control of the situation. Then Mr. Baker had grabbed the sister and he knew the power had shifted in the wrong direction. Now two guns were aimed at Mrs. Baker and he could not allow her death. With expert skill, he had immediately raised his gun and aimed it at the most visible target, Mr. Baker's head, which he could see clearly through the kitchen window. He had then squeezed off two rapid shots, paused long enough only to confirm the target having been neutralized, and then run at top speed from the neighbor's yard to his car parked three blocks away.

Now he started the engine, knowing that the police were likely to spread out their search within a certain radius of the house. Even if they couldn't find their shooter, they'd still ask a large number of the neighborhood residents if anyone had seen a strange person or vehicle in the area, particularly since Mr. Baker had been a high profile, wealthy citizen. So what if he had been indicted for drug trafficking. The cops would still want to pin the rap on someone as soon as possible.

He'd have to ditch the car to be prudent, assume that someone may have noticed it and eventually describe it to the police. He was reasonably certain, however, that no one had seen him, not that he was worried about being identified since he was completely dressed in black and wearing a black baseball cap pulled low to shield most of his face.

Leaving his headlights turned off, he drove out of River Oaks, stopping only once when he saw swirling police lights speeding toward him. Luckily, the squad cars turned a block up the street before reaching him so he vigilantly continued his getaway. His first stop would be a used car parking lot that had a few junkers. He'd exchange this Chevy Malibu for whatever heap he found before daylight broke. Then he'd go to the police station and wait while also monitoring the police scanner for any updates on Mrs. Baker's condition and arrest status. He couldn't predict what the police might do since she had threatened one of them with a gun, but never pulled the trigger. It seemed safe to assume that she would at least make bail so he needed to be present if she walked out of the police station.

He decided to contact his client with the update. "I've located Mrs. Baker," he stated matter-of-factly when the man answered his phone.

"Well, that's no surprise!" the man scowled. "The whole damned world has located her. She's on her way to the police station as we speak!"

"I'm on my way there as well." He turned onto a street named San Felipe and headed east in search of a car lot.

"For what? We don't need you and your sloppy methods anymore."

"But I –"

"I'm sure it's safe to assume that you're behind Mr. Baker's untimely demise?"

"Sir, the subject was about to shoot Mrs. Baker and my orders were to keep her –"

"Your orders did not include killing Mr. Baker! You may have just ruined everything!"

"Sir –"

"As far as I'm concerned, your ineptitude is without match. Rest assured that I'll be speaking with your superiors about your inferior work!" He hung up.

Once again, the operative battled with anger at his client's ignorant insolence. He rapidly redialed the man's phone number several times, but no one answered. Now he gritted his teeth, unable to prevent the fury from washing over him, succumbing to the malice that invaded the calm disposition that was his trademark after so many successful years in his line of work.

His client was a fool, an amateur! And even worse, he was planning to ruin his career with no thought to gathering facts. He couldn't allow that to happen. He would not allow it!

The unusual tide of emotion flooding his mind initiated an overload that jammed the synapses firing off in his brain. Like a crashing computer, his mental display screen was frozen and his internal circuitry demanded a cold reboot so that he could think logically. Obeying the commands from the frontal lobe of his brain – his figurative hard drive – the operative abruptly wiped his mind clear of the thick anger clouding his judgment. He then slowly began to allow facts, not emotions, to trickle back into his brain for assessment, for a course of action to be determined as he continued driving down San Felipe. Self-preservation always took precedence over any other agendas, assignments, persons, or monies at stake or in conflict. His client had been unwise to threaten the flow of his future assignments and there must be repercussions for the man's arrogance. He could assume that his final payment would also be withheld, but money was not the motivator now. There was only one necessary, reasonable line of action, he decided. Very soon his client would be sorry to discover why and how he had earned his exemplary reputation in the field.

—⁂—

"So now I'm corrupt," Harold stated flatly as he sat down across the table from Mona, who was still handcuffed. He set a hot cup of coffee before her, but she refused to touch it as she glowered at the detective. They were the sole occupants in the interrogation room, but she guessed that Nate or some other detectives were probably listening in from a small room behind the mirror on her right. "Why do you think that?"

"I want my attorney."

"He's on his way, Mona, but does he need to be here before you tell me what I've done to make you distrust me." His voice was pleasantly calm, but his eyes betrayed the concern.

"You set me up to get killed, that's what you did!" she spat.

"Set you up?" Now Harold's confusion was fully evident on his face. "I think you've got me mistaken for your dead husband. All I've ever done was try to keep you alive."

"Bullshit! I know you're on Aaron's payroll. Or maybe the Escobars's."

"Okay, you're so convinced that I haven't been straight with you, tell me what I've done, Mona." He glared at her angrily. "And this had better be good."

"You sent a cop to guard my hotel room knowing that he'd conveniently disappear so one of your other buddies could try to shoot me in bed."

"What a load of crap!"

"And you never got any quote-unquote suspects at the hotel who aided the killer, probably because you're the one who masterminded the whole setup!"

"I was the one who tracked down the identity of the asshole who broke into your room!"

"Yeah, and you supposedly traced him to a drug dealer who you never found!"

"God." Harold abruptly jumped to his feet and paced the small room.

"And when that didn't work, you called me at Jocelyn's house so I'd leave."

"I also called you when Aaron was on the way back home so you could get out of the house before he arrived!"

"Only because you wanted to blow me up!"

"What kind of sense does that make? Are you listening to yourself?" Harold was overwhelmed with frustration now.

"Pardon me for not being able to think like an assassin, Harold," Mona forcefully continued. "I just assumed that you couldn't risk Aaron going to jail for murder and ending the payoffs you must be getting from his drug operation."

Harold finally stopped pacing and stood stark still to face Mona with complete disbelief. "How could you get me so wrong? And why would you think that you'd be improving your situation by becoming a murderer?"

"I was thinking about my child, Detective. I certainly couldn't rely on you or any of your other cop friends, could I?" Mona stared at him, her eyes bloodshot with emotion. Oddly, she wasn't afraid of what could happen to her anymore. She felt like she was holding the aces with Harold, who was working really hard to cover his ass right now.

Harold walked to a corner and stood facing the wall while rubbing his right hand over his jaw. After a few seconds used to regain his composure, Harold seemed deflated when he again approached Mona. "All I can say is that I'm sorry you felt you couldn't trust me, Mona, because I thought we'd at least gotten past that issue." He again sat down across from her at the table. "I'm also going to inform you of another fact you've gotten wrong. We did locate the drug dealer, a guy named Antonio Suarez."

Mona froze at hearing the name Antonio, struggling to keep a straight face.

"We just got a call yesterday about his location, but it was too late to do us any good."

"Why was it too late?" Mona almost whimpered, hoping that Harold's response wasn't the one she dreaded.

"Because he got himself killed in Galveston a couple of days ago. Right now we think it was someone working for the Escobars because the junkie he hired to kill you at the hotel didn't get the job done." Mona's stomach dropped as she wordlessly stared at Harold, who continued with the police's theory. "The word on the street is that Antonio fled Houston hoping to find you before the Escobars found him. He thought that if he could finish the job of killing you, then the Escobars would be satisfied and leave him alone."

"Oh."

"Strange the way he died, though. I can't share the details, but he had some very odd injuries. Someone found the body dumped by the side of the road yesterday and called it in."

Mona lowered her eyes to the table to prevent Harold from seeing the guilt that she felt.

"Anyway, it's too bad we couldn't get him alive because he would have been a link to Aaron, the Columbians, or whoever wanted you dead."

Mona wanted to confront Harold about whether the link would be to him, but the wind had swiftly retreated from her sails upon her realizing that the police might eventually tie Simone to another murder. She wondered what would happen to her sister, who was probably being interrogated in another room even now.

—⁂—

"You just don't know how to stay out of trouble, do ya?" Nate was sitting across from Simone in another interrogation room down the hall from the one currently occupied by Mona and Harold. "We were prepared to offer you a get-out-of-jail-free card if only you could keep your freakin' nose clean." Nate cruelly stared at Simone, who remained silent. "Frankly, I'm glad that you screwed up because I think you belong in prison. You shot your uncle in cold blood like some common crackhead. And look atcha now, dressed like the whore that you always were. You probably wanted your uncle to give you a little something when you were a kid, didn'tcha?" His cold eyes mockingly played over Simone's overexposed body.

Simone was too angry with Nate to trust herself to speak so she was left to cast her eyes to her lap, where her cuffed hands were clutched. She had never met a cop that she liked, but she'd also never been at the mercy of one as despicable as Nate. Her instincts screamed at her to deliver a sharp kick to his groin, his leg, something beneath the table, but the effort would have been futile under the circumstances. She swallowed hard and reflected on the fact that her future was over and she would probably be subjected to people like Nate for a long time to come behind bars. Anything could happen if she was locked up. She could be raped by female inmates, shanked for a bar of soap or a tampon, anything. The idea of living out the rest of her life in such hopelessness caused the indignation she felt toward Nate to promptly flee her body. "What do you want from me?"

"Ah! She finally speaks!" He smugly pushed himself backward in the chair, tipping it back slightly on its two rear legs. "Well, for starters, I wanna know who got the bright idea for you to murder Mr. Baker tonight. And who was the third shooter that fired into the house when Mr. Baker took aim at your sister? My bet is that it was one of your hood friends given your history. I want a name."

"I don't know who it was. All I know is that neither I or Mona killed him, Detective. Didn't the cops at the scene tell you that?"

"I'm the one asking the questions here, got it?" His chair dropped to all fours again and he crossed his arms over his chest. "So whose idea was it to kill Mr. Baker tonight? Yours? Your sister's? Or your shooter friend's?"

"I don't know what you're talkin' about." There was absolutely no reason for Simone to cooperate with Nate since her life was over whether or not she answered his questions. He had already alluded to the fact that she could count on being charged with Clarence's murder. Now that she understood the fate that awaited her, she numbly went mute, going inside herself as she had done so many years ago whenever Clarence had forced himself on her. It only made sense to do so now since Nate was enacting another form of rape, that of her human-ity and her dreams. Suddenly, she was a teenager again, lying on her back and staring blindly at the ceiling as Clarence invaded her body. As Nate continued with his antagonistic interrogation methods, her being took flight to a distant universe where she was safe and un-able to feel anything remotely painful. Her mind regis-tered from somewhere that Nate was nearly yelling at her, but it was okay. She was okay. He couldn't harm her now as she floated among the shooting stars and willed her soul to blast forward like a bolt of lightening. She wanted to travel alongside one of the rocketing comets and spin in summersaults with freedom. Life was good after all. And she wasn't trapped or cornered.

Simone began to hum an old childhood favorite, "This Old Man," as she cruised among the fiery stars surrounding her. She was untouchable now and she was actually glad to have returned to her soul's playground after so many years of absence. It was good to be back here.

After Simone had been humming for a few minutes, Nate pressed his palms flat on the table between them and leaned forward to stare into her vacant eyes. He then waved a hand in front of her face before standing straight and turning to look at the large mirror on the wall. "Somebody call a damned doctor."

—⁑—

Harold was suddenly called from the room, leaving Mona with her thoughts and fears about Simone, their future, and Sophie. If she were booked on murder conspiracy charges, she'd be put in jail, which meant that Toots would have to keep her child for longer than any of them had planned. And poor Sophie was bound to be worried when she awakened in a few hours only to find that her mother had not returned as promised. If only she could call Toots! But Mona just couldn't risk it. She couldn't risk anyone finding out where Sophie was until she knew that her child would not be in jeopardy.

Before leaving the room, Harold had continued with his questioning, but to no avail since Mona had firmly decided to say nothing else until Richard arrived. She hoped that whoever was standing behind the mirror facing her had gotten an earful of her accusations of Harold's corruption. Then again, it probably didn't matter since whoever was watching was bound to be part of his crooked circle of accomplices. She heaved heavily, dispirited and frightened as Harold reentered the room.

"Got some bad news. Your sister is being taken to the hospital."

Instantaneously roused from her despondent mood, Mona nearly leapt from her chair. "Why?"

"Mental breakdown. She lost it while being interrogated."

"What do you mean she lost it?" Mona didn't believe Harold's characterization of her sister. There had to be more to it. "Did one of your buddies rough her up or something? I'm telling you right now that if anything has happened to my sister, I'm going to slap your department with the biggest, most public lawsuit you've ever had!"

Harold seemed to be taken aback by Mona's hostility. "It's not like that. Nobody touched her, Mona. She just lost it, went Twilight Zone on Nate from what I've heard. The ambulance is here now and she's going to the hospital."

"Can I go?"

"No, you can't." The fervent remorse in Harold's eyes was almost tangible. "I wish you could, Mona, but we've got too many unanswered questions to let you go."

"Are you going to book me?"

"It looks that way, yes."

Richard was abruptly escorted into the room with his briefcase. He astutely nodded at Harold before rushing to Mona. "Are you okay?"

She frantically shook her head. "No. Simone is being taken to the hospital right now and I'm stuck here with no way to be with her." Frustrated tears began to roll down her cheeks, but she was unable to effectively wipe at them since her hands were still handcuffed. Upon noticing her physical restraint, Richard was immediately incensed.

"Detective, take those handcuffs off my client immediately! You know that she is no danger to you or anyone else here!"

"Sorry, counselor, but the cuffs stay. It's standard procedure since she held an officer at gunpoint earlier tonight."

Richard's eyes flew to Mona's face. "Yes, I heard."

Mona merely looked away without responding.

Richard sighed. "Very well. Then if you don't mind, I'd like a moment alone with my client."

"You've got five minutes." Harold went to the door, hesitated long enough to take one last look at Mona, and then walked out.

Richard assumed the seat across from Mona that Harold had formerly occupied. "Mona," he spoke soothingly, "I want you to be mindful that there are people watching us from behind that mirror, alright?"

She nodded and sniffled at the same time.

"Good. Now tell me exactly what you've already discussed with Detective Monroe."

—⁂—

The five minutes that Harold had allotted to Richard and Mona was fleeting, but the attorney had nevertheless managed to gather just enough information to formulate a different story designed to get his client released tonight. When Harold returned with Nate to the interrogation room, Richard immediately stood and straightened his suit coat. Mona had already been instructed to refrain from any further statements.

"Detective, I'm going to insist that my client be released immediately without further delay. You have no grounds to keep her here."

Harold reacted with the expected surprise. "And just how do you figure that?"

"Do we need to remind you that your client threatened to shoot an officer tonight?" Nate appeared ready to lunge at Richard. "I swear, you lawyers will say and do anything to get your guilty clients off. Anything for some dough, huh, bud?"

247

Richard was unfazed. "Quite to the contrary, Detective, it is your department that will say and do anything to get my client killed."

"And just what the hell is that supposed to mean?" Harold placed his hands on his hips as the door opened and Captain Perez entered the room. Mona's eyes nervously hovered between all the persons in the small space, but she kept silent as ordered.

"It means that we have evidence that your department is either dangerously deficient or exceedingly corrupt, having grossly failed in each of your supposed efforts to protect Mrs. Baker from persons who would otherwise have her killed. And we are prepared to press charges against the Houston Police Department for your apparent willingness to enable her death."

"That's the most ridiculous thing I've ever heard!" Nate almost did lunge at the lawyer now, being restrained by Harold's strong arm as Captain Perez stepped in front of the detectives to address Richard.

"Mr. Wilkes, I'm sure you realize that your assertion is not only inflammatory, but cannot be proven. These two detectives have gone out of their way to convince Mrs. Baker to accept police protection for herself and her family."

"And what happened when she did accept the protection, Captain? May I remind you that your officer allegedly took a restroom break – or so he says – just before a would-be assassin broke into her room and tried to kill her?"

"The man had to pee!" Nate's unflagging support of Officer Costello's lapse spurred Richard's next comment.

"And this sort of camaraderie among your officers, even in the face of obvious incompetence or corruption, serves only to further prove my point, Captain. Your department is begging for a lawsuit and I'm inclined to satisfy that need because every honest, private citizen relying on the lot of you is at risk."

"Richard, we're considering booking Mrs. Baker on charges of attempting to assault an officer and conspiracy to kill her husband," Captain Perez coolly responded. "What does that have to do with your crap about police corruption?"

"Allow me to explain. Mrs. Baker had a prearranged time to meet with Mr. Baker yesterday evening so they could amicably discuss the status of their marriage and his indictment. It would seem, however, that Mr. Baker forgot about their plans and went out for the evening. He later returned home with a woman who just happened to be Mrs. Baker's sister, who had never met Mr. Baker and would not have known prior to their arrival at Mr. Baker's house that her companion for the evening was actually her brother-in-law."

"That's a pretty damned big stretch if I ever heard one!" Nate was turning beet red while everyone else in the room, especially Mona, listened with stunned silence as Richard spun an imaginative tale that smartly challenged the policemen's much more accurate version of the events.

"Meanwhile," Richard evenly continued, "Mrs. Baker was disappointed at missing Mr. Baker earlier so she also returned to the house in the wee morning hours only to discover your officers holding her husband at gunpoint. At this time, she didn't yet realize that the other woman present was her sister."

"What a crock of shit!" Nate threw his fists up in the air and stared with sheer disbelief at everyone in the room. "Is anyone actually buying this crap?"

"Quiet, Detective," Captain Perez calmly raised a hand toward him without moving her eyes from Richard's face. "Go on."

"Because Mrs. Baker believed that the policemen were complicit in their efforts to have her killed, she immediately assumed that the officers were now attacking her husband with plans to murder him in cold blood. When she drew a weapon on your officer, she believed she was protecting her husband from a dishonest cop."

"How do you explain the fact that the gun was unregistered?" Captain Perez's tone revealed no prejudice as Nate gaped at her and Harold.

"Mrs. Baker is no expert on guns and would not have known that the seller was less than savory or that the gun is illegal."

"And who was the seller?" Captain Perez raised an eyebrow.

"An unnamed man who we'll probably never hear from again, Captain. It was a private, random sale outside of a pawn shop."

"I see." Harold thoughtfully rubbed his jaw, his demeanor having become much more subdued as Richard had outlined his assertions of police corruption and Mona's innocence. "You don't think we'll be able to trace the gun to anyone who could implicate Mrs. Baker for deliberately purchasing an illegal weapon. Which also implies that we can't prove her criminal intent."

More agitated than ever, Nate drew closer to Richard, but remained blocked from direct contact by Captain Perez's watchful eye. "So you expect us to believe that Mrs. Baker actually wanted to reconcile with her husband, showed up at two o'clock in the morning to get it on with him, and decided to kill a cop who was trying to save his life?"

"We believe that this police department is overrun with crooked officers who are accepting payoffs from hoodlums around the city. These same officers had everything to lose if Mr. Baker seemed willing to expose his knowledge of their illicit activities. It is our assertion that Mr. Baker did in fact plan to expose these officers' corruption, intentions that he communicated to my client before he was killed. Apparently, the wrong people got word of his plans and got to him first. We believe, Captain, that one of your men is probably the mysterious shooter who killed Mr. Baker tonight."

Nate pranced around the room, speaking to no one in particular. "I can't believe this guy is alleging that with a straight face!"

Both Captain Perez and Harold ignored him. "And what evidence do you have to support this line of reasoning?" Captain Perez seemed genuinely intrigued.

"Right now, we have only speculation, but my guess is that a thorough investigation will implicate someone in your department if you get your people on it. In the meantime, I have advised my client to abstain from any further statements in her current state of distress. Any information she may have provided to you prior to my arrival should be considered coerced and uncorroborated. And I'm sure that you can understand that with her sister in the hospital, Mrs. Baker is in no condition to entertain more questions at this time. If you insist on interviewing her tonight, you will receive no benefit for your efforts and I can guarantee that a lawsuit will be filed against this police department for your blatant negligence, ineptitude, and apparent corruption as soon as the courts open in," he glanced at his watch, "in three hours. And I might add that the press could learn about your officer's suspicious restroom break at the hotel."

Captain Perez crossed her arms over her chest. "Are you threatening to leak confidential information that could jeopardize our investigation, Richard?" Her own veiled threat was written in her grim expression.

"Captain, you know better than that. Should any damaging information get into the media's hands, it certainly would never be tied to me." His point was lost on no one. Richard would obviously be the source of any headlines of police corruption, but he was smart enough to cover his footsteps.

Captain Perez sourly wrinkled her brow. "Counselor, as clever as you think your fairy tale sounds, I'm reasonably certain that a jury would laugh in your face. At the very least, I've already got all I need to lock her up for the attempted, aggravated assault of an officer whether or not we ever prove murder conspiracy. And unless she has a gun permit, I can also charge her with the illegal possession of a firearm. Now, I'm willing to bargain if she'll come clean. If you really want to help Mrs. Baker, you'll tell her to talk."

All eyes were now on Richard as he met Captain Perez's gaze without flinching. "Captain Perez," he stepped toward her and lowered his voice, "I think it would be a good idea if we discuss this matter privately. I have some information that I'd prefer not to share in so much company."

The captain paused briefly before nodding. "Fine. We can talk in my office." They both went to the door and Richard opened it as the captain turned to Harold and Nate. "I'll be back in a few."

—◊◊◊—

Captain Perez's "few" seemed to Mona to be a few hours as opposed to minutes. While they waited, Nate had slunk back to a corner and seethed while leaning against the wall as Harold and Mona wordlessly sat. From time to time, their eyes met and Harold seemed on the verge of saying something, but then he looked at Nate, who was watching them both, and remained silent. For once,

Mona was actually glad for Nate's company because she wasn't interested in hearing anything that Harold could possibly think to say in the face of all the danger she and her family had suffered over the past week. All she could think about, all that mattered, was the condition of Simone and the immediate fate of her daughter. Finally, after an eternity of waiting, the door swung open and Richard returned with the captain.

"Mrs. Baker," Captain Perez crossly began, "we're going to release you so you can go to your sister in the hospital."

Mona nearly yelled as the air in her lungs rapidly escaped with her relief, but the strength to stand had yet to reach her legs.

Nate leapt toward the captain. "What the hell is going on here? This lady tried to kill a cop tonight! Are you actually letting her get off for that?"

"Nate, there's more going on than I'm at liberty to discuss with you. You'll have to trust me on this."

"But Captain –"

"That will be all, Nate." The captain met his angry gaze with impatience before turning her back on him to face Mona.

"Well, so much for justice for all!" Nate stormed out of the room and tried to slam the door behind him, but the door was equipped with automation that resisted his fury, easing the door closed in slow motion as everyone watched.

Richard smiled self-assuredly at Mona before turning his attention to Harold. "Detective, please get those godforsaken handcuffs off my client."

Harold didn't budge, casting a confused glance toward the captain.

"Go on, Harold. Take 'em off. Mrs. Baker is free to go."

Choosing to bite his tongue and follow orders, Harold quickly crossed the room to Mona, who now stood with her wrists held out in front of her. Once the handcuffs were removed, he and Mona shared a lingering look, his eyes filled with curiosity, her eyes filled with guilt and guarded relief. Mona rubbed her wrists as Richard placed a firm hand on her shoulder.

"We're going to check out your attorney's story, Mrs. Baker. Expect that we'll be in touch with you and Miss Edwards with additional questions. Your attorney has assured me that there will be no more disappearing acts." Captain Perez was facing Mona and Richard with her back to Harold, who looked on with obvious astonishment. Mona could only nod speechlessly before looking up at Richard once more.

"Come on." Richard opened the door. "I'll give you a ride to the hospital."

—⁘—

When they were safely in Richard's car and on the way to the hospital, Mona finally asked, "You wanna tell me what just happened back there?"

Richard snorted with a half-smile without taking his eyes off the road. "My dear, I cannot reveal all the details, but suffice it to say that I've been in a position as your husband's former attorney to accumulate a wealth of information that the captain would be loathe to have made public at this particular time."

"You mean that she's been taking payoffs? She's part of the corruption?" Mona's stomach grew queasy with the understanding of how high up the problem went.

"Everything is not always so simple. The most I can say is that Captain Perez is in a spot that implies her knowledge of the good and the bad within her department."

"And she refuses to do anything about it because she benefits from it."

"I didn't say that."

Mona was abruptly irritated with her attorney. "Why are you being so goddamned cryptic?"

"What difference does it make? The most important thing is that you're free. Wouldn't you agree?"

"Hmm. For what it's worth, I guess. I may be free, but I'm not safe. And neither is my family."

"Actually, you may be wrong there. I tend to think that Aaron's permanent retirement has probably solved your problems."

Yes, Mona thought to herself, that had been Simone's expectation. She looked out the window into the night. She could hardly wait to see her sister.

—m—

As soon as Mona arrived at the hospital and checked on Simone, who was sedated and deeply asleep, she found a payphone and called Toots. It was approaching eight o'clock in the morning and Sophie was not yet awake, but at least Toots would be able to answer the child's questions about her mother's whereabouts when she did eventually emerge from her bedroom. She hardly dared to hope that their lives would transition back to some semblance of normalcy now that Aaron was gone and the threat of a trial exposing his drug partners had been alleviated.

Too weary to eat, Mona eventually returned to Simone's hospital room and sat beside the bed as her sister slept. She gazed at Simone's peaceful face for a few moments before grasping her sister's soft, small hand. A strong hand despite its size. She would never let her sister go.

"Hey, I don't know if you can hear me, but I want to tell you that I love you more than you can possibly fathom. You are my dearest – maybe my only – friend and the greatest sister a person could ever ask for. Thank you for loving me enough to come back into my life and to help me the way you have. I owe you a tremendous debt. And don't worry about going to jail. Richard took care of us tonight. When you wake up I'll tell you how to answer the police's questions." She placed Simone's limp hand against her cheek and continued looking at her sister's tranquil face. Quite unexpectedly, she felt Simone gently squeeze her hand although Simone's eyes remained closed and her facial expression didn't change. Mona gathered that Simone had mustered just enough energy to let her know that she had heard her before slipping back into her peaceful slumber. Exhausted but refusing to release her sister's hand, Mona lowered her head down on the bed near Simone's stomach and drifted off to sleep.

FIFTEEN

Mona had waited a couple of weeks, lying low at Toots's condo with Sophie and Simone before marshaling the guts to return to Houston. During this period, she had taken a small gamble at trusting Detective Monroe again, allowing him limited information of her where-abouts once all threats of police charges had ceased. He also left messages on her voice mail regarding the word on the streets these days, addressing Mona's on-going concern that there might still be policemen or Columbian drug traffickers wanting her dead. To ev-eryone's relief, Harold claimed to be hearing from his informants that the worries of her damaging testimony had been quelled now that a trial was not forthcoming and Mona, who had fallen conspicuously quiet of late, had no further cause to help the D.A. Although Captain Perez had seemed unsettled by Mona's charges of po-lice corruption, there had been no investigation to her knowledge for reasons that she could only guess at with an increasingly dubious opinion of the Houston police force.

It had actually been a stroke of good luck for Mona that a yet unnamed assassin had killed Aaron because no one was prompted to avenge a murder that had no identifiable proponent or executor. Meanwhile, Harold confided to Mona that the Escobar operations had resumed in the city, stimulating his suspicion that Aaron's replacement had already been installed. Unfortunately, the honest cops were back at square one in terms of identifying and building a case against this person.

Sad, terrible news had reached Mona on the same day that Simone was released from the hospital. Mere hours after Richard had so gallantly and eloquently rescued her from the police's interrogation, he had been found shot to death in his home office. No one knew who would have had reason to kill him and nothing had been taken from his house. Mona suspected the police, of course, since Richard's death had occurred shortly after his threat to expose their corruption and sloppiness, but, like Aaron's death, Richard's demise had been ruled practically unsolvable as no clues had been left behind. Shortly after the murder, his young wife had moved out, saying that she simply could not sleep in a house that held such a painful memory. No one could blame her.

Having returned to the River Oaks mansion that she had once shared with Aaron, Mona now lay in her own bed, restless and dissatisfied. Although glad to be back in a house she had considered home for nearly a decade, she just could not get comfortable within the walls, experiencing similar feelings as Richard's widow. But Mona would not relocate. Rather, she would change the walls, shift some guts in the house to reflect a different, new mood that did not remind her so much of Aaron or his gruesome murder. She had already hired an interior decorator to redo his former bedroom, which was the largest in the house, and to redesign the kitchen. She had not yet decided whether she could ever sleep in Aaron's room again, but she would reserve that decision for another day once the decorator had worked some magic.

Mona glanced at her clock and noted the time: a little after two-thirty in the morning. She had been unable to sleep for some reason since around midnight, her mind unusually active, grasping for wisps of something that wouldn't quite make itself known. It had been this way since she moved back into the house and it was wearing on her nerves. Mona had thought that taking a new lover very recently would have given her a physical justification to fall into a weary sleep, but even this strategy had failed to outwit her mind. Even now, her latest acquisition stirred beside her in his sleep, a new experience for her, having a lover who actually slept with her all night. He was different from any lover she had ever known, different in ways to which she had not previously been receptive, a testimony that this relationship might be more serious than she was yet willing to admit to herself. She reluctantly accepted the fact that she enjoyed having his hand on her stomach as he slept. Mona placed her hand atop his and gently rubbed it, feeling his skin and appreciating how much larger his hands were compared to her own. Succumbing to his overtures to sleep over had been a giant step for her, one that he couldn't possibly understand since he seemed so naturally open-hearted and open-minded, qualities that she fully lacked. But she must be changing somehow inside because she had surprised herself by opening her bed to him rather than insisting on trysts in neutral locations as she had with past lovers. It was a start anyway.

Perturbed, Mona gently tugged his hand off her body and got out of bed to stand at her window in her white silk nightgown. From here, she had a decent view of the front lawn and the houses across the street, a peaceful setting that she had always found pleasant. But tonight she expected to see something more, something that just wasn't there. She struggled with the images dancing around the edges of her mind, growing extraordinarily still and losing herself in the struggle. She felt like she was losing because she was trying too hard so she relaxed, peering out of the window and letting her gaze drift to the fountain in the front yard. The fountain. Water. Water. Something about the water. Suddenly, a long dismissed detail bolted into her brain and her mental sight observed a different body of water. Mona could hardly believe it had taken her this long to figure it out! Sure of her suspicions, she reeled on her bare feet and hurried from the bedroom without bothering to don a bathrobe or house shoes.

Mona knew that she was right when she plunged headfirst into the warm swimming pool water. There had always been a loose brick in the right-side pool wall near one of the lights in the center. When Mona's and

Aaron's marriage was new and their relations genial, she had tried reminding Aaron on a few occasions about getting the brick fixed, but he had always shrugged off her entreaties as unimportant. Really, she hadn't cared since she didn't like to swim anyway, but the pool had seemed to be Aaron's prized feature on the property so she couldn't understand why he wasn't interested in better preserving its immaculate structure. Now she thought she knew.

Mona swam down to the area where she remembered the loose brick. After nudging a couple of places, she finally pressed on the right one. Out of breath, she quickly surfaced for more air, inhaling deeply before sinking back under the water to pull the brick from its corner near the pool light. She then thrust her hand into the space left by the missing brick until she felt something beneath her touch. Detecting a thin metal handle, Mona grabbed it and pulled her potential trophy from the hole, soon after surfacing breathlessly and energetically climbing out of the pool.

Without any wasted seconds, Mona examined the gray, metal box she had found, her wet gown clinging to her body, exposing her nakedness underneath. The box was somewhat small in terms of dimensions, measuring perhaps eight-by-eight inches. Clearly, Aaron had grown complacent about anyone ever discovering the box after having hidden it in the same place longer than Mona would ever know. The top wasn't even locked, quickly popping open when Mona pressed a small button that was fitted with a missing key. She dropped to her knees, subconsciously catching her breath as she opened the box and found a sealed plastic bag, which she promptly removed. Anxious, she pulled apart the seal, revealing yet another plastic bag inside the first. She now pulled open the second plastic bag and stared at the contents. In the poor patio lighting, she couldn't make out much so she tipped the bag over and let the contents drop onto the ground. That was better. Now she could see that there was a bank statement for an account in China as well as a small blade with Chinese inscriptions on the finely jeweled handle. There was also a debit/credit card for the same bank noted on the statement, undoubtedly for the same account. This had to be the drug money that the police had wanted her to find! She excitedly stared at the bank statement without understanding what she was seeing. Before she could calculate the amount of money in the bank account, Mona would need to find out the exchange rates for converting Chinese currency into American dollars. With her sketchy knowledge on the subject, she was unwilling to guess at how many millions she had just discovered.

"I believe that you're looking at my paycheck, Mrs. Baker. Put all the documents back in the box and hand it to me."

The voice was vaguely familiar, not one Mona had heard more than once, but a spear of fear pierced her heart. She heard the click that she recognized as originating from a gun thanks to Simone's training, but this information was no good if she had no way to defend herself. Without yet turning to face her adversary, Mona began to obey his command, gathering the bank documents and restoring them to the metal box. The Chinese blade had fallen just beside her foot and it was the last thing she slowly grabbed. Pretending to lift the closed box up to her opponent, Mona slowly turned around, still on her knees, and raised her hand upward to present him with the box. He was dressed entirely in black and wearing a black baseball cap, but she still recognized him from the Target parking lot. He was the same man who had saved her from the car bomb and later thrown her to the hot asphalt when she'd tried to free herself from his grip. He was a spook, accustomed to controlling whatever situation in which he found himself, but Mona wasn't going for it tonight. There was no way she would allow this jerk to just walk up and deprive her of the treasure. She briefly wondered if the money had been his impetus for helping her that day, but now was not the time to try to piece together the puzzle. While he was distracted with grabbing the booty, she let out an Amazon-like screech and plunged the blade to the hilt into his left calf as he let out his own savage yelp of pain and went down beside her, dropping his gun in the process. Before he could grab her, she yanked the knife out of his leg and placed the blade against his throat, crawling on top of him without any thought to her basic nudity against his body.

"Make one move and I'll cut you from ear to ear," she panted with a sinister glare. She stared directly into the man's eyes and considered stabbing him even if he obeyed her.

"Hey! Freeze! Get up!"

Mona's gaze bolted upward to her lover as he ran toward them with his gun pointed at Mona's captive. He had obviously thrown on his pants in a panic, having failed to zip his fly. Luckily, he had fallen asleep in his underwear so the flagrant fly would not present a disagreeable situation.

"Harold –" Mona started to explain what had just happened, but the unidentified man used the moment to wrestle the knife from her grip and fling her off him. Before he could stand, however, Harold took aim and shot him in his arm, forcing him to release his grip on the knife. The man then reached for Mona's neck, but was too late because Harold was already standing over him with his gun pointed at his head.

"I said freeze!"

Mona scurried out of the man's reach as he lay paralyzed on the ground beneath Harold's gun. Finally motionless, he stared up at Harold, who immediately kicked the knife a safe distance away from them.

"Mona, call the police. Tell them you have an intruder and that I've subdued him. And make sure to also tell them to send an ambulance." He glanced at Mona for a quick second. "We're gonna have a talk, lady, about this violent streak you've developed."

—❦—

Before the police arrived, Mona collected the metal box and stored it inside her house. While Harold continued to hold the intruder at gunpoint on the patio, she dressed in a pair of jeans and a sweatshirt, her clothing selection these days having undergone a dramatic change since having her life jeopardized several weeks ago. Somehow the importance of blending in with her wealthy neighbors had been shed during the ordeal. Mona hated the analogy that constantly sprang to her mind – a snake shedding its old skin – but maybe that's what had happened in some way.

To minimize the trauma of the intruder's presence to Sophie, Mona told the child to stay in her room until otherwise instructed. She promised to later explain what had happened to Sophie, eliminating most of the details, of course. According to the child psychologist that Sophie visited each week, Sophie was doing well coping with the death she had witnessed in the hotel that fateful night. She had come a long way in recent weeks and Mona had vowed that nothing would jeopardize her daughter's progress.

The man had refused to answer any of Harold's questions, choosing to remain completely mute while they waited for the other officers to arrive. As Mona rejoined them, the police and an ambulance arrived so she again left Harold with the man to open the front door. Shortly afterward, she led the EMTs and officers to the patio, whereupon Harold relinquished custody of the man, pointed out the location of his gun on the ground, and explained what had happened to the best of his knowledge. Mona also gave a statement, conveniently leaving out any mention of the metal box and its contents as the man was handcuffed to a gurney and shuttled through the patio gate to the driveway. The EMTs would rush him to the hospital for the surgery necessary to extract

Harold's bullet. It would be a while before he eventually made it to the jail.

Harold had by now collected his shirt and was buttoning it as he leaned down to kiss Mona's cheek. "I'm going to the hospital to try questioning this guy when he's out of surgery. Will you be okay?"

"Yeah, I'll be fine. Thanks." A sparkle lit her eyes as she looked at him, but then quickly dimmed and went out. She couldn't change overnight.

"So what's with that box you hid in the house?"

"I'll tell you about it later."

Harold stared questioningly at her for a long moment before, "Alright. I'll wait. I know it's not easy for you to open up." He turned and walked toward his car parked in the driveway. "I'll call you later."

"Okay." Mona watched as he lowered himself into his car, started the engine, and drove away. For a split second, she thought she already missed him, but she didn't. Did she?

She went back inside, returning to the box, which she had placed in the library upstairs. Before she could do anything with the money she had just found, she would have to know what her mysterious guardian-slash-killer said to the police during questioning. She already knew that Harold would tell her when he called later that day.

—◆—

It was nearly noon and Mona was waiting on pins and needles for Harold's call. Thankfully, Sophie was at school so she didn't have to banter with her daughter while she waited with tense distraction. When the phone eventually rang, it was Simone, not Harold, calling to tell her about the job she had accepted and to wrangle a commitment out of Mona to visit her with Sophie for Christmas – without Harold. Simone didn't like cops, even if her sister had decided to give one of the louses a chance. So be it. Mona didn't even know if she'd still be seeing Harold by then. Christmas was a long two months away.

After talking to Simone for a little while, Mona was again left to wait, not allowing herself to start counting her newfound millions until she was certain that the police wouldn't be trying to confiscate the money.

She was anxiously lighting a cigarette when the phone rang again and Mona jumped up to read the caller ID. It was Harold.

"Yes! Harold, what's up?"

"Boy, you've got way more pep than I expected."

"I've been waiting for you to call."

"I thought you might need to get some sleep so I waited a little while."

"Augh! I haven't slept a wink since you left and you know it! Now tell me about this guy."

"Alright already. He's not talking so we had to run his prints to ID him. His name is John Mackie and he's a former Navy Seal, dishonorably discharged for getting caught with dope he said wasn't his around five years ago. Claimed he was set up by an officer who hated his guts, but he couldn't prove it. After leaving the Navy, he disappeared. My guess is that he's been working as a mercenary since then. We ran ballistics on his gun and got a match for the weapon that killed your attorney a few weeks ago. The weapon also matches the bullets pulled out of Aaron's skull so it looks like we've got our guy."

"I don't understand why he would kill either Aaron or Richard! He kept me from getting blown up at Toys'R'Us so I thought he was hired to protect me, not kill anyone."

"Well, maybe he killed in order to protect you."

"Nah, that doesn't make sense. Richard was no threat to me."

"Not that we know of, anyway. We've gotten the phone records for his cell phone and this guy was talking to Richard for a week before Richard was killed."

"Really?" Mona began to pace as she mulled over this revelation.

"Really. I think Richard may have hired him to protect you, but I can't figure out why yet."

Mona thought she knew why. She stared at the metal box. There were probably several million reasons. Richard must have been waiting for her to find the money so he could get his dirty hands on it. He must have also been the culprit who planted the cocaine in their house and phoned in the tip to the cops. Lord knew he'd certainly spent plenty of time in her home and would have needed just one opportunity for Aaron to turn his back. So now Mona understood how Aaron could have been set up to be put out of business. She also understood Richard's motive – the money. He had been obliged to keep her alive once the police had commissioned her to locate Aaron's secret stash, which Aaron had neither discussed with anyone nor disclosed the location of despite how they may have tried to gain his trust. That still didn't explain why Richard's hired help had murdered the crafty attorney, but the reason had to be linked to either greed or stupidity or both.

"You sure are quiet." Harold sounded concerned. "Do you need me to swing by? Need some company?"

"I'm fine. After everything that's happened lately, I feel like I can handle just about anything, Harold."

"Yeah, I saw that thing you did with the knife last night. I've been meaning to talk to you about that."

"There's nothing to talk about. It's a part of the new me. I'm not the same woman you met at the police station in September."

"So who are you now?"

"I don't know yet, but I'm looking forward to finding out."

"Well, I'd like to find out with you if there's room for two on the adventure."

Mona touched the metal box and pushed the button that opened it. "So tell me, what do you know about China?"

—⁓—

He would escape. It was just a matter of time and his proficient watchfulness. All he needed was one opportunity. These cops might think they knew who they were dealing with, but they didn't really have a clue. John scoffed inwardly at their ultimate ineffectiveness.

He had always been the best, capitalizing on every survival and killing skill he had learned in the Navy. And the cornerstone of it all was patience, waiting, just waiting for the perfect shot, the perfect cover, the perfect slipup of his enemy while maintaining superhuman inertia, exercising static as opposed to kinetic energy. Not one of his fellow Navy Seals had been better at it than he had been.

The sniveling Navy officer, Martin Keller, who had planted dope in his locker years ago had been seething with jealousy at how quickly John was moving up in the ranks. So quickly in fact that John had been up for his third promotion within as many years when he'd been forced to resign from the Navy. Once discharged, John had waited for around two years before exacting his fatal revenge on Keller, who had gone out for a beer one night and never been heard from again.

Sequestered in his hospital room, John quietly observed all the activity, already memorizing anything that seemed routine, focusing on his goal to identify the mistake that would set him free. Once he escaped, he had every intention of visiting Mrs. Baker and collecting the payment his former client, Richard Wilkes, had foolishly decided to deny him. For Mrs. Baker's sake, John hoped she was indeed as smart as she had recently shown herself to be. He would hate to torture her for the money. But he would definitely hurt her, take her to the brink of death if he had to.

Mrs. Baker. Having her practically naked body on top of his by the pool last night had ignited a sense of the manly erotic needs that John had learned to suppress.

The complications that tended to arise with women just weren't worth the trouble, he'd convinced himself while in the Navy. But Mrs. Baker seemed to be different. He had watched her closely for a week and been subjected to her brutal potential when she threatened to cut his throat. Now that he thought about it, he admired her a little. She was no simpering wimp like most women, who would have cowered in a corner and bawled until he'd left rather than fight for something they wanted. Maybe he and Mrs. Baker were alike. Maybe he didn't need to kill her for the money. Maybe they could join forces – on several levels.

John pondered Mrs. Baker for only a few more moments before returning his attention to the activity outside the hospital room. The policemen posted outside his door were no match for his proficiency. All he needed was for someone to make one small mistake that he could use to get free.

Krys Batts is a Texas native who has spent the last thirty years writing creatively. Her novel, What's Done in the Dark: A Mona Baker Novel, is the first in a planned series of mystery novels.

Krys currently lives in Dallas, Texas. Visit her website at www.krysbatts.com.